Penny Rose

Annette Stephenson

*A*cknowledgements

To my loving husband Brent, whom I give all my love to. You have always believed in me and my talent. For your inspiration, I am forever grateful.

To my children, Oliver, Jacob, and Kamara. From the first day we met, we fell in love. Thank you for your friendship and my grandchildren.

To my parents, Jimmy and Elizabeth. Thank you for bringing me into the world enabling me to show my true colors. I wish you were here to see how far I've come.

To mentors and faithful readers who love these stories. We adventure together on journeys that take us to places like no other.

\

Prologue

London Taylor was not your average detective. He spent most of his career shooting for the stars, trying to solve the hardest cases he could get. It started off well as he turned a mediocre business into something lucrative. Exposing cheating spouses, hiding out, and uncovering evidence was the part of his job that he was good at. It helped that he was very good at photography. While developing his own pictures, his smarts often figured out who were true humans and who were heartless liars.

But after ten years of successfully cracking cases and establishing a reputation, things changed. London was tired of his routine. He was getting less sleep from nights camping out in his car, waiting for a small-time culprit to surface. Following the unfaithful spouse felt less fulfilling. Subjects were always guilty until his research proved otherwise. He had developed a sense that made him cunning and sly. He could feel things in the air. Excitement used to be out in front, while fear lurked behind him. In his imagination, he could see someone's boyfriend appearing around a corner and ending his life for being someone who should have minded his own business. Investigating was what he knew and he wanted no other career. Quietly stepping inside his own meager apartment revealed his own shortcomings. He would have never operated his business that way. Strewn newspapers and clothing littered his room. All he could do after a long night was to fall asleep in his clothes, without eating. Could it be that the business had taken its toll on his body and mind? As he lay on his bed, he realized it was time to make some changes. If he were asked last year to think of giving up what he once enjoyed, it would have been a far-fetched idea. He loved it so much. It had been a good fit because he didn't sleep well at night. He was also lonely. The friends he knew well were those he worked around. They were useful for information, like Sullivan Banks, who was a former reporter until he qualified to anchor. He had many years of experience to draw on.

London never made time for vacations or organizing his apartment. It always looked like a tornado swept through his home. His mind occupied with strategies; he had little time for a girlfriend. That was fine with him. He knew his work would complicate any relationship.

A bar had recently opened down the street from his place. He passed by it a few times, deciding it would never fit into his schedule. Realizing that he had kept to himself far too much, he reasoned it might be a good change of pace.

The sign outside announced the headliner, a singer named Penny Rose. After entering, he felt relieved. It wasn't one of those smoke-filled bars, keeping a nasty bowl of nuts behind the counter, touched by every hand coming out of the bathroom. It was more like a small nightclub he could come to when he needed a good drink to relax with. It was dark, a soothing kind of dark that would make him want to stay late into the night. London ordered his favorite drink, a Stoli, his choice in Vodka. He carefully limited his drinking and avoided wine. His line of work kept him on the alert and he began gauging the individuals inside, the lonely husband, the business partners, the party goers, and couples who just needed a night out.

Before he was served, she stepped onto a low stage and soft lights focused. When she lifted her microphone, all fell silent. With a smooth voice, Penny Rose mesmerized everyone in the room. She knew what she was doing. Most patrons were men with a significant other, but it was easy to see that mostly gentlemen were intrigued with her performance. She was sensual and sultry without acting sexy.

From the bar, London noticed Penny's eyes. She read the room like a pro. Toward the end of the song, she fixated on him. Was she trying to enthrall him? He felt her entrancing pull. Then she closed her eyes, touched the microphone, and whispered her lyrics. The lights dimmed as she ended her melody. There was a brief stillness and then she bowed her head. The audience applauded.

London turned away briefly and took a swallow. It was indescribable, like nothing he had ever experienced. His eyes followed her as she slowly stepped off stage in her black dress and heels. The people at the closest table invited her to join them and bought her a drink.

London was suddenly curious. Who was she? What was it about her that intrigued him? She quietly took another sip, then lifted her head. Their eyes met and London turned away. He told himself that it was natural for any man to look at and listen to such a talented soul. He wasn't obsessed with her, that would be childish. Besides, she was in a different league than he was. He began wishing he had checked the place out days ago when she first arrived.

The bartender was busily wiping the countertop and putting away glasses. London's instinct was to quiz him. After all, he was good at getting facts and compiling a dossier.

If only he knew that the woman who took his breath away could profoundly change everything for him, if she let him in. Penny Rose was more than a woman singing in a bar. She was a deeply troubled person needing a way to escape from what was trying to kill her. London had no clue as to what was in store for him and what was about to change his life.

Chapter 1

Loneliness Doesn't Care

There wasn't much to do after a long stakeout in the city. He walked in as the sun peeked between tall buildings and electrical wires. Hearing birds awaken at daybreak made him jealous of their good night's rest. Wiggling the door key into his deadbolt, he noticed another newspaper in front of the door. He had canceled that subscription months ago but they kept coming. He scooped it up and threw it on the pile by the recliner. Opening his fridge, he was reminded that he hadn't been to the market in a while. He cracked open the last Coke and poured it over ice. Turning on the morning news, he hoped it would lull him to sleep for a few hours.

Even though he worked occasional nights, he also liked to keep busy during his days by developing photographs, answering emails, and messages. It was not much of a life, but it was what he knew. He should have been blessed with a family of his own and a wife to love for the rest of his life. It was his own fault. He never made the time to get to know anyone who might accept his way of life. It did not help that his parents had been killed when a driver hit them head on. He consoled himself, remembering how he visited and helped out when they needed a hand. They never had to ask; he just knew. Then it happened. It was a blow to have to bury the two people who shaped his life and instilled the hope to succeed in any venture he chose. His parents saw it in him as a child. When he was young, London was always interested in the art of intrigue, hidden clues, and scavenger hunts. Just using his imagination wasn't enough.

If his parents could see him that day, would they be disappointed? He started hating his work and his life, losing the will or courage to improve it.

"The same old horrible news," he thought. Bored with TV, he took hold of the remote control and turned it off. A sleepy cat padded out of the bedroom, stretched and yawned, the hint that he was ready for his morning meal. KB the cat, was a stray that found London during one of his jobs. There was no other choice but to take him home and nurse him back to health. After two weeks, he acquired his name. When London sat at his computer, the cat demanded attention by jumping up and sitting on his keyboard while he worked. It was harder to type but they grew used to each other. The poor thing was found dirty, cold, and hungry. London didn't know if he was really ready for the responsibility of caring for a living thing, but he couldn't turn away. Each time he would see him curled up near the window, warm and fed, it was a reminder that he must have done the right thing. KB just felt appropriate.

Checking his calendar, he realized Sullivan was stopping by that day. They had met years ago and worked on investigative pieces together. At that time, London used an anonymous name as a cover and started calling his friend Sully. It just sounded like a nickname suiting a newsman who got the job done. He quickly learned that Sully was the best in the business, only to retire a few years later. They stayed in touch ever since.

After taking a hot shower, London toweled off, wrapped the towel around his waist, and looked through his closet to find something that might fit his mood. Most of his clothes were darkly colored. He had style but thought negatively about it. His room wasn't much to look at either. He felt no need to decorate with a comforter and lots of throw pillows. Sleeping most of the time away from home, he just needed a mattress and flat pillow. He threw the blanket over and tossed his only pillow toward the head of the bed. The pile of dirty laundry in the corner always missed the hamper and the washer. It was an annoying chore to him. He just had better things to do. Looking in his drawer, he noticed he had one pair of clean socks left. He finally resolved to do some laundry later. He didn't require much in the way of home life. He owned a few pots and dishes and most of his drinking glasses were mismatched. He could see small nail holes in the wall that were never patched by the previous tenants that still needed paint. He called the place a hole in the wall and a place to hide. Whatever his reasoning, London didn't plan to go anyplace else. He didn't want to connect it, but it reflected his mood.

A couple of years ago, he settled on the location in the city. At the time, its best feature was that it was affordable. The older building housed several apartments that always had something needing repair. The landlord did what he could to fix what was broken and treated him kindly. London never thought he would live in an apartment like it. It was not how he was brought up. Even though he got his Bachelor's Degree in Education, he never used it, assuming he would be no good at it. Instead, he decided to use the money he saved to open his own agency, Sloane Detective Services. Still grieving over the death of his parents, the business would have gotten off to a rocky start if he had not accepted help from others who knew the industry. Eventually, he hired employees and a bookkeeper. After eight years, his faithful employees were let go and he kept his accountant, making life simpler for the time. He was growing tired of constant requests to investigate minimal cases that weighed him down. It disappointed him that his choice to be an investigator grew less inspiring. What happened to what he built?

He was glad that Sully was coming to visit. Maybe he could shed some light on what was going on in his head.

"Hey, Lon. I see the place still looks the same as last week. Why don't you clean up?"

"I made my bed," he said confidently.

"I'm not impressed. I bet I could find dirty socks under that bed." He knelt down to pet the cat.

"You could be right," London admitted.

"Hey, KB." He paused to add a comment. "What a weird name for a cat. You should have given him a cool name like that cat in the Runaway Bride movie. *Italics*, now that's a good name for a cat."

Sully could smell coffee brewing as London opened the cabinet to get the mugs.

"It's good to see you again. Did you come to give me advice on how to housekeep or lessons on stupid pet names?"

"You know I never need an excuse to come by. But I am worried about you. What's going on?"

"I think I'm just in a slump. I had to follow another guy whose wife suspected that he was unfaithful. I submitted the pictures to her and she said she had to file for divorce. There is something about these cases that makes me feel dirty and disgusted. Just another plain and boring case. It wasn't supposed to be this way when I started out." He opened the fridge to search for creamer. The container was empty.

"What did you think investigators do? You've been in this business long enough to know what it cntails. You get some simple ones and you get some complicated ones. Work goes on. Something else is happening with you."

London's face changed as Sully tried to figure him out.

"I still have a box of my dad's stuff. I went through it again yesterday. We were a good family. I just keep seeing how much my parents really loved each other and then they died together. I still really miss them."

Sully did his best to show compassion, "I am sorry that happened. Your parents were good people but we can't change the past."

"There's nothing I can do to change how I feel. I don't really have a life here. My parents left me

11

their house but I can't live there. It's too big and it's just too hard to go inside."

"You know, I still miss the good old days when you and I worked together. Remember the Johnson job? That was a scary one."

"I remember. I was full of fire back then."

"You are still very good at your job. You seem to be busy."

"I had a few good cases lately. They paid well."

"That's good. You know, London, when I was young, being involved with the news was something I never thought I would give up. Now here I am, retired and all I have left are memories of a long career. You don't want life to pass you by like that. Before you know it, you'll be old like me."

"I hear you."

"I hope you do. Take it one step at a time. I'm sure you'll figure it out."

The cat slowly walked over toward London and rubbed against his hand.

"On your way over, did you see the new bar? I thought about checking it out when I'm not on duty," London remarked.

"That's a good start. Get out and enjoy life a little. I know losing your parents makes you feel alone. But you always have my support. Seriously, getting out for an evening will loosen you up."

London pondered on it for a moment and began to like the idea. He needed to push himself and take a break from his loneliness that was only magnified by being shut up in a tiny apartment. What would it take to change who he had become? When he was younger, he had exciting adventures. Sully encouraged him to not give up on his business, or on life.

"You know, I think I will give it a try. Do you want to join me tonight?" he invited.

"No, thanks. I plan to spend time with my daughter and new grandson. He's growing so fast and I feel like I'm missing out."

Sully walked over to where the old newspapers were piled. He gathered them up and stacked them on the counter.

"I gotta go. Recycle these. It could be the start to getting this place clean." He waved his hand around as he walked toward the door.

"I'll get on it. Thanks for coming by."

"You take care and call anytime if you need to. And Lon, give the cat a new name," he said jokingly.

London shook his head and began to chuckle.

"Bye," he shouted from the kitchen.

London felt better. Trusting a friend who was good at listening eased his mind. Sully was older and felt like a father to him. London got started on the dishes and took his trash out. Dirty laundry went into the machine and he turned on his computer.

During the day, he loved working from home. There were times when he worked in daylight following individuals. He was always amused how clueless they were of their future. After giving his clients the results, he collected his fee and moved on. He preferred not to think of them again. There was always another case on the horizon. London spent the day looking at surveillance cameras and running background checks. He had a keen eye for recognizing suspicious and questionable activities. Sully's words kept coming up in his head about how good he was at his job. It was true. Some days he felt like a champion who could reveal the truth and relieve the innocent one who was being cheated on. He also admired Sully's happy family life. London hated to admit it, but the fear of being alone scared him a little more each year. He wanted to end that loneliness so badly and yet it felt out of reach.

Finding new ways to hide out and take photographs was challenging but it was the kind of work he loved. He had a good resume and years of experience. So why was his passion shifting? After settling his parents estate, he drove by their home. London avoided getting out to look around at the emptiness left behind. The gardeners he hired to care for the landscaping were doing a good job. But going into the house he grew up in was still too painful.

On his way home, he was rethinking his career and where it was going. He was better than that and hoped to get out of the funk he had fallen into. If only he could get back to the way he used to be when he first started out. Sully was good for London. He needed to know he could go to someone to help him sort it all out when it became overwhelming. All those years, he made a difference in the lives of others. Whether it was good or bad, he worked hard to get to where he was. But something had to change and he had no idea what that would look like.

He gathered up the old newspapers to put in the recycle bin. Maybe taking time for himself was a good plan to help him feel good again. He even thought about cooking a meal for a change and skip the drive thru.

In the meantime, he needed to make a difference in someone's life, something with meaning and purpose. Little did he know that opportunity would arrive sooner than expected.

\

Chapter 2

The Red Fedora

Steven Morris opened a new bar a few weeks earlier, The Red Fedora. The neon sign with a flashing hat hung above the entrance. An A-frame stood outside the building with the words, "Live Music" painted on it. The vacant building had sat empty for years. After investing in another restaurant downtown, Steven decided to renovate the old building and make it a nighttime watering hole for patrons wanting a taste of classy nightlife. His buddy owned a bar back in Chicago and hired singers to entertain. That wasn't Steven's original plan. His business model was to hire the best bartenders and upsell drinks. He also wanted to serve appetizers instead of large menu items. The money was in the mixed drinks and fine wines. As the renovation progressed, he began to envision a stage and performer. After some research, he discovered it really would bring in more customers and keep them inside for another round. More people meant more drinks. If it worked, return patrons would fill his bar nightly. It was then that he decided to hire someone to perform at his establishment. As entertainers answered his ad, he started the vetting process. He realized how many talented and experienced singers were looking for a paying gig. Duets, musicians, and one comedian auditioned. Steven knew a piano player, Sasha Barron, who agreed to help with the tryouts. He was known as a talented songwriter who played concerts in his day. At seventy years of age, he still had what it takes to be a professional artist.

"This is harder than I thought. I can't decide who is right for this job," Steven complained to Sasha.

"Did you narrow it down to who fits the mold?"

"Most of them are good. I'm not cut out for this kind of thing. Bartending is so much easier. You just hear people's problems, give good advice, then you call them a cab and send them home."

Steven slapped the auditions on the counter and sighed, running his hands through his hair in frustration. He wanted someone before the bar opened that night.

"Don't stress it. It may not happen tonight. You'll know it when you hear it."

Sasha tried to sound positive. He would love to accompany a unique and beautiful voice with his piano. Before the bar opened, he would sit and play some of the pieces written when he was younger. He never liked the silence of an empty place. Everything woke up when music filled the air. His hands touched those keys intimately, giving listeners a reason to return for more.

An hour later, a woman walked into his place, wearing an open dark coat and sunglasses. Black gloves up to her elbows complemented her form fitting dress and heels. Brunette hair flowed softly over her shoulders. Steven couldn't help but admire her. Sasha smiled as he observed Steven's expression.

"Can we help you, Miss?"

"I'm here to sing for you. I'd like to audition."

"What is your name?" Steven asked.

Her beautiful red lips spoke her name tenderly.

"Penny Rose."

The men looked at each other and Sasha nodded his head. He could see a seasoned performer.

"Interesting. A stage name?" Steven implied.

"No," she answered emphatically.

"Well, okay. You can begin when you're ready."

Sasha sat at the keys as she walked on stage. She gracefully removed her coat and approached the microphone. She whispered to Sasha her song choice and key. He knew it. Before she opened her mouth, the men could see that her stance and presence was phenomenal. Her voice came out clear and with perfect pitch. The sultry tone of her vocals made Sasha grin. Steven had to admit to himself it was the best he had heard so far. She wasn't frightened of the stage, which made it easy for her to give her best. When she finished, Steven and Sasha were stunned.

"That was incredible. Where did you learn to sing like that?" Sasha asked.

She just looked at the men without answering.

Steven broke the silence, "We can let you know. Is there a number where we can reach you?"

"No. Do I get the job or not? I want your answer now."

"Steven checked with Sasha, who shrugged his shoulders. Then he gave him a cue to give her the job.

Steven quickly announced, "I think you are a perfect fit. Be here tonight at seven."

"Thank you, gentlemen," she said. It was her only reply as she walked to the exit, draping her coat over one arm.

"Is it me or was that unusual?" Steven scratched his head, a little thrown back by her demeanor.

"I think you found your singer. I will happily play for a woman with that much class and talent."

That night, the place filled up slowly and orders for food and drinks began coming in. In the back, Penny was getting ready to perform an array of songs she was fond of and good at. Sasha had his list ready to accompany her. Customers had no idea what to expect when they saw her walk on stage. The lights dimmed and all they could see was the silhouette of a woman, beautiful in form. When Sasha announced Miss Penny Rose, he began to play. The room quieted and they watched intently. When she began, patrons stopped whispering to each other. Her tone, style, and vocals were beyond professional. It wasn't another amateur that just walked into a bar, she was putting on a show. Everyone enjoyed listening. She sang for two hours with a break in between. When she was through, customers waited around, hoping to hear another set. Penny walked up to Steven, mentioning to him that she would be back the next night and held out her hand. He gave her an envelope with cash inside.

"Thank you," she nodded and quietly left the bar.

"Do you ever wonder why she never says much?" Steven inquired.

"Who cares? She did a great job and that is what you needed. She helped you bring in a lot of money tonight. I haven't worked with a good singer in years. This is a dream for me," Sasha said, feeling good in his heart.

"Well at least you have a conversation with me. I guess it shouldn't matter."

Penny Rose got into her car and drove home. She was actually living with a friend who used to work for the Secret Service. As she walked into the condo, his curiosity was piqued.

"Your first night, how did it go? Until now, people around here never knew about that voice of yours, except me," Joe commented.

"I never thought I would get to sing again. For now, it's a good place to keep a low profile."

"So far, you seem to be safe. Dressed like that, they shouldn't find you there."

"They're not that stupid." She threw her keys on the table and plopped down on the couch next to Joe. "They're looking, I know they are. I keep it quiet around the bar and watch my back as I leave. I don't want anyone to catch on."

"You sure look the part. I thought you hated lipstick."

"I do. It's just a cover. For now, I have to forget who I used to be. For how long, I don't know."

"Here, I poured some wine for you. Relax a little. We worked this out and I think we were wise. I haven't seen any problems so far."

"Don't count on that. I know they're still looking. I've changed my hair, my name, everything is different. This is no time to let my guard down. I am glad they didn't ask for ID or references at the bar. Steven pays under the table. So, it's perfect."

"I told you I would lend you money if you needed it."

"No, thanks. You've been kind enough to keep me here. I still hate to involve you. I fear for your life. You already risked everything to keep me safe."

"Just stick with the plan and we'll be okay."

After taking off her makeup and thinking about the role she played, Penny Rose reflected on her life before getting involved with the man who kept an ugly secret. At night, she was the singer at The Red Fedora, as long as she stayed low. If only she could gather enough information to put Mason Banks and his men behind bars. She was the key to getting justice and proving her innocence. Until then, she would watch her back, making sure no one knew her whereabouts or guessed what she knew.

Joe was a longtime friend and like a father. When he learned of her story, he wanted to protect her and keep her out of prison. He was fired from the Secret Service for not revealing her location and information about her involvement with Mason. She appeared to betray the FBI and let her guard down, playing the part of someone she wasn't. She had done it with prior cases and exposed evidence without getting caught. Mason was the type of man who cared less about life and more about money. Penny knew that. Because she pretended to join his criminal plot, she was regarded as a traitor by the force. It was a serious act against her loyalty to her coworkers. No matter what she did to prove herself, no one believed it was part of a larger plan. She was forced to do it without the support of those who believed in her. When her situation grew precarious, she needed to get out. At the time, no opportunities surfaced for redemption. She was on her own and all she had was Joe to back her up. She quietly cashed out her savings and investments, which had slowly depleted.

In her former job, Penny had traveled the world, easily hiding behind varied hairstyles and makeup, was skilled with concealed weapons, and spoke four languages. But before that, she put everything into a career that didn't involve working for the government, singing.

Because she insisted on bringing down the most hardened mastermind out there, she had lost it all. She and Joe planned it out methodically. It had been a few months since they disappeared and she became someone else. Joe moved her away from Europe to California under assumed names. Living a normal life without being recognized was a continual challenge. Even though she kept quiet, she loved singing at The Red Fedora. It brought back memories of her past when she performed as a skilled vocalist in her younger days.

Penny Rose wasn't exactly sure how she would prove her innocence without the US government backing her. The sun would need to shine from the one person she needed. That person was London Taylor.

Chapter 3

Should I Trust You?

London recalled what helped him make his career choice before his parents died.

His campus was filled with young hopefuls wanting to turn their training and skills into rewarding careers. London had focused on education. He believed that inspiring students being their best was a good way to make a difference. After going back and forth with aspirations, London won the argument with his father and left home to chase his dream. It was everything he thought it would be. He did the things college men did, late nights with the guys and short relationships with girls. After graduating, he spent a lot of time applying for positions searching for young, dedicated teachers who understood their students.

Things changed suddenly when his childhood friend Craig, was killed when men robbed him as he got in his car after work. It was a random act and no one was found, accused, or tried for such a terrible crime. His friend was a helpless victim, waiting to be forgotten. It took away all of his faith in justice. His father, John, was understanding and had friends in the police force. He related his own story about finding justice in the world, being an important factor when trying to reason with London why bad things happen to good people. It became an obsession at first for London. Someone had to care. It was hard to have the answers to every incident. His dad's world revolved around his family. It was important to spend time with the wife he loved so dearly and a grieving son who missed his friend.

No one ever caught the man who killed Craig. Like his father, it tortured London. He seriously considered becoming an attorney. But it meant he would have to defend crooks and that was definitely not for him. He decided to join the police force. He was good at interrogation and getting answers. After attending the academy, working as an officer for two years, and taking a college course, London qualified as a criminal investigator. It was hard work and stressful, but it was satisfying. He could do something that strengthened him through his effort. He was known for his degree of training and absorbed as much as possible from his senior officers. London especially enjoyed getting confessions from the guilty. The possibility was always in the back of his mind to find the man who killed his best friend. He didn't care how hard he had to work to put the bad to rest, it was worth it. Sleepless nights were riddled with visions of the incident. He wanted no one to experience what he went through. He fine-tuned the business of asking questions and pushed the envelope until he got answers. He recalled a conversation with his father.

"What's going on, son? You look tired," John observed.

"Sometimes it gets to me. I have been doing this for a few years and it seems to never end, like chasing my tail. Years ago, someone got away with taking the life of a good son and friend." London felt like he had been overexerting himself over Craig.

"I know it still hurts, but you will have to put it to rest sometime. We do all we can to protect those who deserve it, but it doesn't work all of the time. All we can do is try and hope that it improves the circumstances for someone."

"I need to do more than that. Putting it to rest is not easy for me."

"Yeah, I get it. You've been that way since you were young. You hated to see anything harmed. You brought back so many bugs and animals hoping to save them."

"Somctimes I think about going back to teaching."

"Is that what you really want?" John questioned.

"I'm on the fence with it."

"You've already done so much for justice. Look at what you have accomplished in the name of Craig. Your passion actually did some good." He put his hand on London's shoulder and squeezed. "Whatever you decide, make a wise choice, one that gives you purpose and feels rewarding. I'm sure you will choose what's best."

London appreciated everything his dad was doing for him. Close and supportive, he sensed his father's faith. It was obvious that he was growing tired of chasing injustice. But was his passion still inside? He couldn't help but admit he loved investigating, but law enforcement tied his hands with rules and bureaucracy.

After his parent's accident, he relived all of the keepsakes they kept in their cedar trunk. They had saved everything of London's including a scrapbook of his accomplishments. Yearbooks, pictures of family gatherings, report cards, and fishing trips were memories that showed his parent's pride in him. His father was his mentor, best friend, and supporter. Even though his mother, Allison, cherished him, she loved watching her husband be a good father. In her eyes, no one cared for a child more than John.

It was a shocking loss that ended London's world abruptly. News of his parents death sent him into a dark place in his heart. At the funeral, he leaned on Sully. At an earlier banquet for families of officers killed in the line of duty, he was introduced to him. The older man attached himself to London and shared his love of investigating.

After his shower and shave, Sully's words came back to mind, enjoy life. He should get out and take some time for himself. He dressed in his best and liked how he looked in the mirror. He was handsome, fit, and wearing his favorite cologne. With a confident style and a full resume, he wondered why he held back finding love and having a family. He was definitely not interested in finding love in a bar. That was the last place to look. After giving his cat a rubdown, he stepped out his door. It was around seven-thirty that evening when the street lights highlighted the mist in the air. He parked around the corner and locked his car. The street was wet and his leather shoes left tracks behind him. It was the first time he had pulled them out of the box since he bought them. Walking up to the door, he could hear the piano. It was warmer inside. It still smelled clean and looked new. He casually scanned the room. It was a habit. The conversation was punctuated by a laugh and he noted that everyone was dressed a little nicer. The pianist ended his melody and the lighting changed. Everyone's attention quickly centered on the stage. They knew what to expect.

London sat at the bar where Steven put a napkin on the counter for him.

"What can I get you?"

"Stoli, neat."

"You got it."

She appeared on stage and placed herself in front of the microphone. Her head remained down until soft notes played. Smoothly, she began a moody rendition of an older tune. He sat there for a moment and listened. She was gifted. The piano and her voice were in perfect harmony and it was soothing. A glass landed on the napkin.

"Been here before?" Steven asked.

"No, it's a nice place."

"Thanks. How do you like our entertainment?"

"I think it's a nice touch."

"You haven't seen anything yet. My customers love her."

As she continued, London wondered how such a talented woman ended up at a local bar. Then she looked directly at him. Maybe it was just a part of the show. When she sang through a few sets, she sat at a table near the stage where customers gave her compliments. Her eyes kept searching the room. When they met his, she rose and walked over. She approached the bar and stood next to London.

"Dark, red Merlot, please," she said as she pushed a loose strand of her hair behind her ear.

"That was a good performance. I don't know how you do it."

She glanced at London as she took a sip.

"You're new here, aren't you?"

"How did you know that?"

"I see regulars in here almost every night. You are a newbie. You don't look like the other stuffed shirts here."

He eyed her as she touched the rim of her glass.

"My friend encouraged me to get out and relax more. I should introduce myself. My name is London Taylor."

"Penny Rose."

"Interesting name."

"So, you needed a nudge to come here? Well, welcome." She noticed what he was drinking.

"Is that your preferred drink?"

"Yeah. I guess I just settled into a comfortable spot. I'm not big on change."

"So, you're comfortable?"

He chuckled, "Excuse me?"

"Comfortable. Settled and no longer exploring your options. Not even trying what our innovative bartender can create for you."

"I just don't see any reason to change a good thing, including my beverage."

"Well, touché!" Her tone changed and she felt flirtatious. He could sense it as he watched her wet her lips.

"You seem to have mastered the art. Have you performed at other places?" he asked.

"I guess I've entertained my share of audiences."

"Was it your first choice as a career."

"It's a preference."

"I'm pretty good at reading people. You have a way about you that intrigues me." He was using his investigative skills to unveil more about the songstress.

She was caught off-guard and tried to sound casual, "What do you mean by that?"

"There's a lot more to you than singing."

"Now, how would you know that?"

"Because of what I do."

"Which is?"

He whispered, "I'm a private investigator."

Surprised by his answer, she took her last sip and walked away. She grabbed her coat in the back room and headed back for the bar where Steven was.

"Penny, did I say something wrong?"

"Sorry, I have to go."

"I apologize if I offended you. I wish you would stay."

"Enjoy the rest of your evening, London Taylor."

She walked up to Steven, who put her money on the counter. They both watched her leave quickly. London was puzzled by her way and asked Steven about her.

"What do you know about this Penny Rose?"

"Not much. She's quiet, not the kind of person who has a long conversation. Occasionally she talks to customers briefly. She's good for business and that's all I care about."

"She was friendly. Strange she left so suddenly."

Steven blurted out, "Hey, just don't get any ideas about dating her. She's very reserved."

"No, I'm not interested in her that way. She left in a rush when I told her I was a PI."

"Maybe private eyes make her nervous. What are you thinking?"

"It's just an opinion, but I think she's cautious. I won't judge without knowing what she's really about. I could be wrong."

"I just mind my own business." Steven took her empty wine glass from the counter and moved away. London felt no reason to stay. He left a tip and walked to his car.

Parked away from sight was Penny, waiting for him to come out. She had to admit that she enjoyed talking to him but knew she shouldn't trust anyone. As he drove off, she followed. Penny was used to spying on suspicious people and he wouldn't suspect her at that distance.

When he got out of his car, he had his keys in his hand. She took multiple photos and different profiles of his face. She used binoculars and found his apartment as his lights turned on. She calmly drove away, checking her rear view mirror. Was meeting a detective just a coincidence? What were the odds of meeting an investigator who entered the bar? She trusted no one and would take no chances. It was just too close for her comfort.

"You're home later than usual. Where've you been?" Joe worried.

"I spent a little time at the bar. I met this guy that came in for the first time. There was something curious about him."

"I hope you're not having romantic ideas. You know where that got you last time."

"It's a cover and no, I'm not looking for love."

"Did you probe and find some answers? You know, you've always been good at knowing who to trust. Did your instincts prove to be true?"

"While talking to him, I felt like he was on to me. Then he dropped a bomb on me."

"What bomb?"

"He's a private detective."

"Whoa! Do you think he's one of Mason's guys?"

"I don't know. I followed him home. I got several pictures and his address."

"I hope he didn't see you."

"Of course not. I'm good at hiding. Remember, I used to be an agent." Emotion showed in her voice.

She unzipped the back and slid out of her dress. She threw it onto the bed, put her hair in a ponytail, and pulled on an oversized hoodie.

"That's more comfortable."

"What should we do next?" Joe asked her, knowing what her response would be. It was in their nature to research people.

"I need to find out more about London Taylor. Something just doesn't seem right about him. He was pleasant and didn't act like he was after anything. But I know suspects can be cunning and deceitful. His body language was not typical of Mason's men. I still have to be careful."

"That may not be his real name. Some PI's have alias names just like you," he added.

"We'll soon find out."

She immediately began an intensive search.

In his small, dark apartment, London was bothered. Why was Penny upset that he was a PI? He could see that she was hiding her natural reactions and showed a subtle nervousness. He took off his shoes, loosened his tie, and dropped into his chair. Opening his laptop, he started a background check. There wasn't much to go on. He couldn't find a birthdate, address, or history. After an extensive search, he found nothing at all. It was odd, but he suspected the name was an alias or stage name. It was a challenge to crack open and he became more interested in who she was. Curiosity led to more unanswered questions about this woman. Why was she interested enough to talk to him? It sounded like she was upselling the bar's drinks. But there was something more about her that he couldn't put his finger on. His mind kept picturing her beauty and he tried to avoid getting caught up in her appearance. That was his second rule as an investigator. London wondered if he went back to the bar, would she avoid him? He was used to suspects ignoring him and not answering questions. He wanted to take the chance. There was something about her that made him think of a victim or a wanted criminal. If his instincts were right, he might be taking on the most dangerous case in his career.

Chapter 4

Take My Hand

London showed up at the precinct where he used to work. His buddies didn't mind if he used an office for investigations. He perused the wanted list looking for Penny Rose or anyone matching her description. Frustration built up as he kept hitting road blocks. His only recourse was to go back and see her even if it made her uncomfortable. He actually enjoyed it. He was pursuing an inspiring case and admitted it lifted him out of his slump.

The Red Fedora was packed out more than usual. London nervously slid into a small booth. How could he avoid confrontation and a possible scene? He reminded himself to be professional and careful. He ordered an appetizer and a double. He stayed until her performance was finished. That seemed like a good time to try and talk to her.

Surprisingly, after her last set, she walked straight towards him. He put his hand through his hair and took a breath as she neared. She gracefully sat across from him. Her dark eyes pierced into his.

"What are you doing here?" she quietly demanded.

"The bar is open to the public, so you don't need to intimidate. Do you have a problem with me?"

"I guess I just don't like private eyes. They come off nosy and I don't need that kind of stress."

"Are you stressed? You don't really know me. I assure you that I am harmless or do you think I am going to bombarde you with questions and try to flirt with you?"

"I don't need to answer that."

"I apologize. Really, I just enjoyed talking to someone on a lonely night."

"Fair enough. So, what is your track record?"

"What do you mean?"

"Are you good at getting what you want from whoever you are questioning?"

"You could say that. I was on the police force for a few years."

"Was?"

"Yes, was."

She cautiously kept the conversation brief.

She finally spoke up, "Well, I'm done tonight. I'll see myself out."

London lifted himself out of his seat and called out as she neared the bar.

"Can I see you again?"

"It's open to the public. You do what you want."

He was hoping for a longer dialogue, but she intentionally shortened it. She picked up her money and walked out with confidence. London realized that she was trying hard not to act suspicious. He went home perplexed.

The last week, Sully had taken his family on a well-deserved vacation. It wasn't uncommon for Sully to make surprise visits on London and felt an obligation to care for him. Being the closest thing to a father, London wanted to share his latest encounters. It was becoming an obsession to discover more.

"Come on in, Sully."

"It's good to see you. You look different. Are you dating someone?" he asked jokingly.

"Oh, no. I'm not dating anyone but I did go to that bar you suggested."

"Really. It's a nice place. I took my wife there to listen to the music. Kelly loves her voice."

"Yeah, she's pretty good. I got to meet her."

"Do you like her?"

"It's not like that. After she finished, we talked over a drink."

"I think you like her."

"No, she's not my type. Anyhow, how was Hawaii?" he changed the subject.

"It was good. I've been promising Kelly I'd take her and our family on a trip for years. First thing she said was, 'I want to move here.' What a thought, huh?"

"Maybe you can retire there. So many possibilities."

"I hope you don't mind if I bring it up, but have you been to your parents' house recently? I mean, have you gone inside?"

"No. I just park there. I can't take that step, knowing they're not there. Dad bought that house for my mother when they got married. He renovated it and let her put her spin on the décor. They were going to make it their forever home. It's just too hard."

"I get it. If you ever want me to go with you, let me know. Your dad was a good man and I know he had a big influence on you. It's good to know you can look back on your life and know your parents did their best to help you get to this point."

"I feel pathetic. I'm a grown man afraid to enter his parents' home. I keep picturing my mom running out to give me a hug while Dad stands in the doorway waiting to shake my hand and the three of us eating together." Emotions stopped him from continuing.

"I believe you will get your chance to take that step. I know you well enough to see it inside of you."

London turned toward the window and took a breather, his arms crossed.

"What is it, son?" Sully asks.

"Here I am, feeling like a recluse, a shut in. What if I never get that chance to explore a life without them? Recently, someone told me that I am comfortable, too settled. I'm starting to see that."

"Those are things you can always change. I think you are capable of anything you put your mind to."

London realized that opportunity could only come if he let his guard down. He was an assertive and verbal man during his earlier times as a greenhorn. Years had changed things for him. With all his experience, he could take a chance to pull himself off the ground and start new. Sully always had a way of getting to the point without preaching.

Penny reflected on her own circumstances. She used to have friends in the Bureau. Moments came and went when she wanted to call to say that she was alright, doing fine. She was smart enough to know that it wasn't her safest choice. She knew they wouldn't forget her betrayal even though it was not her reality. It wasn't her intention to lie and deceive, she had a job to do. As far as she was concerned, she was still on the case and was not finished until her name was cleared. Determination to prove her innocence occupied her days as she continually searched for evidence. Joe was all she had as far as a friend went. She never planned to involve him, but he was the best at protecting those who needed it, and she needed protection.

After turning up information leading to London's reputable investigating company, she learned that there was no such person as Sloane and learned it was only a catchy business name. Penny spent some time lurking around the neighborhood where he lived. She watched his habits and monitored his timing. No one else came out of the apartment, so she rightly assumed he lived alone. She learned his patterns and followed him to the police station, a coffee shop, and across from a parking garage where he took pictures with a zoom lens. She had to find out if he was hired to find her. Was her life in danger? With so many questions running through her mind, she had to be stealthy.

The next day, London's friend was installing wallpaper in their new nursery and invited him over to help. They thought it would be a good time to have dinner together afterwards. Evan had been married several years and had their first baby on the way. It seemed like all of London's friends were going someplace with their lives. He had always loved babies and getting married was only a future dream. Getting out more and stepping out of his comfort could pay off someday. Driving home, he avoided the street his parents lived on. Visiting the family home was a step too large to take. Anyway, all he could do was park there briefly and drive away.

Penny made her move. Waiting until the neighbors quieted, she silently made her way to his door. Dressed in black gloves and dark clothing, she smoothly picked the lock and went inside. She used her flashlight to search every corner and noticed a cat hiding in the cat tree. London did not appear to be the type to own a pet. The room showed that he didn't have much of a social life. She found his office, a small desk in the corner of his bedroom. An old picture of his parents impelled her to lift and look at it for a brief moment. She rifled through his stacked paperwork and then his files. He kept his certificates on the wall and his cherished accomplishments in the file cabinet. She could read what kind of a person London was. Obviously, he was a high achiever with an aversion to housekeeping. As she went through his computer, she heard noises outside the window. Peering out, two men were talking and one of them was very loud. London's car was still away and that was a relief. She took numerous pictures, sensing that she needed to get out. Thinking he could show up any minute made her hasten her search. As a professional, she had never felt guilty for breaking and entering. After she was through, she tried to make everything look the way it was. She backed out and locked the door behind her. As she slid into the front seat of her car parked in the alley, London came home. She took a deep breath and started her car without turning on the lights. She was used to staying calm when casing an area or building. She needed to assemble her thoughts to find out what the man was all about.

When Penny arrived home that night, she stayed up examining her photos and checking them against his background. An extensive search revealed more details. She inspected his college records, training files at the police academy, and his business portfolio. Never arrested, no previous convictions, no crimes and he was never married. She found the obituary with his parents' names. The newspaper article described the crash that simultaneously ended their lives. She started to see a softer side of London and realized he was just an ordinary man doing what he could to just keep living. His website needed to be updated. She observed that it hadn't been revised since his parents passed. She wanted to dig in and examine what kind of cases he had taken, how good he was at spying, and his success rate. She would have to plan another night in his home to search his closed case files. She needed more intel about the lonely detective.

London placed his hand on the doorknob. Walking in, KB wasn't out begging for attention. Something didn't feel right. He went to his safety box, took out his gun, and slowly checked his surroundings. The desk and papers looked the same but he realized he forgot to turn off his computer. The room smelled lightly sweet, almost like a captivating perfume floating its way through the room. He stepped outside and examined the cars parked at the curb. Nothing. He put his gun away and opened a beer and a bag of chips he bought on the way home. No one had ever bothered him or tried to break in before. His neighbors were friendly enough. They never had issues with burglars or harassment. It made him anxious to think someone may have been in his home. KB was still tucked away in his box. Back in his bedroom, he noticed his file cabinet ajar. Some of the files were mishandled and one particular piece of paper was sticking out of its folder. It was almost midnight. The first person to flash into his mind was Penny. Could it be that Penny Rose was there, in his home? He tried to dismiss the thought, trying not to be accusatory. As he slid under his blanket, he wondered if it could have been her and what did she want? Had she been watching him and would she come again? He decided to bait a trap just in case.

A day later, London went back to the bar for a different reason other than his favorite drink. There she was, dressed in red, wearing a brimmed hat to match her outfit. Dark stockings and high heels made her legs appear long and slim. She grasped the mic to reveal dark red nails, almost a black tone. Her lipstick matched her outfit. When her mouth opened, she mesmerized every man in the room. London deduced if she was that good at seduction, she was capable of burglary. During her next number, she glided off the stage and between the tables. The music and her voice filled the room with what she was born with. When finished, she met briefly with those who gathered around.

41

Minutes later, Penny moved away from the crowd and made her way to him.

"I haven't seen you here lately. What brought you in tonight?" she inquired.

"You."

"Me? Elaborate a little." Steven brought her a red wine as she sat across from London.

"Well, you sing beautifully and you look the part. Is it part of your act?"

"It's not a crime to look gorgeous on stage."

"What kind of a crime are we talking about?" he asked.

"We were not talking about crimes."

"Just think about it."

She acted confused. He was obviously hinting. He reached in his pocket.

"Here, let me pay for that."

"I never let men pay for my drinks."

"A woman who knows what she wants. Clever."

"Okay, why are you really here. Did you fall on your head tonight?"

"I think we have seen enough of each other to act like friends. Do I still make you uncomfortable?"

She adjusted her seat, "No. I apologize for that. There is no need to question my motives. I'm as innocent as they come."

"Really?" he asked under his breath.

Her demeanor was convincing and London wanted to believe her.

A number of people stood up to dance to a slow tune meant for swaying.

"Would you like to dance?" he asked her softly.

"I don't take offers to dance with anyone at this place."

"You have a lot of rules. It's just a dance, not a marriage proposal."

"Oh, so you're offering?"

He grinned and spoke slowly and clearly, "I want you to accept the offer to dance with me."

"Alright, once."

He took her hand and they blended into the crowd. His hand pressed against her back as she drew near.

"You know, you could have your pick of better places to sing. A talented woman like yourself has more class than here, right?"

"Maybe I like the smaller venues."

He stopped talking. A familiar scent registered with him. Penny Rose wore perfume. It wasn't strong, but it was there, misted near her neck. She slid her hand near the back of his head and touched his hair. When she leaned in, he could feel her power against his body. London reminded himself that she was a professional. What was she good at? He knew she was good at getting what she wanted.

He spoke near her ear, "I may not be here for a week. I have to be out of town. Don't go dancing with strangers. I'm not trying to make a move, but I like being here with you." He hoped his detective wiles were charming enough.

"That's a nice compliment but I'm not interested."

"Interested in what? I just like your company."

"You are nice to look at and you can dance," she admitted.

"We're just moving slowly to the music."

"But you haven't stepped on my toes. That's a good sign."

"Oh, I see. So, we can be friends?"

"What kind of friends?" she asked.

"The, we don't date and we don't kiss, kind of friends."

She smiled, "Okay, as long as you remember that I still have that issue with trusting you."

"That should make being friends more fun."

After their dance, they slowly pulled apart. It felt good to be held so closely. She softly touched his face and waved with her fingers as she parted from him. She said nothing more as she left him standing without her on the dance floor and disappeared.

London believed Penny suspected nothing. He had an idea it was her who searched his home. He wasn't stupid, but she underestimated him. He could outsmart most anyone. Trapping her was the best way to find what she was after, if she fell for it.

For a few days, London parked his car away from his apartment, walked in the back way, and waited for a possible culprit. On the third night, he was not disappointed. He accurately guessed her mind was planning something while he was away. Peeking out his window, he could see her getting out of a car.

"Bingo! Right on time." He heard a light sound near his door. There was something he was feeling as he listened. Could it be that it was her or just the excitement of the catch? He wanted answers.

With the lights still off, he sat prepared to give her the shock of her life. He could hear the metal sound of a lock pick and his heart raced. As the door quietly opened and closed, she pulled out a flashlight. Before she could turn it on, London flicked the light on.

She gasped. "Oh, no!"

"You better have a good attorney because you picked the wrong place! Now, are you going to tell me what you are doing hcrc...again?!"

"You figured it out? My guess was right," she said coyly.

"You know I'm a private eye. I'm a proficient clue finder. Your perfume wasn't quite subtle enough. You weren't a very good cat burglar that night. Tonight, I could have shot you."

"I've been in worst situations." She dropped her bag on the sofa and made herself comfortable, he was surprised how calm she was.

He got up from his chair and walked toward her.

"What is it that you want from me?" He added force to his voice. When she did not answer, he put his hand on the side of her face and slowly ran it down her chin. She did not move away.

"You have an answer?" he asked quizzically.

"I needed to know who you are, who hired you."

"And that gives you the right to come and break in? You know, you come off creepy sometimes."

"You were involved in law enforcement and a detective, the best busy body in your craft. I think you were hired to find me."

London was taken aback. His heart was still pounding in her presence. He had to refocus with a line of questions.

"You think I was hired to find you? What evidence do you have to make you think that?"

Before answering, she looked into his eyes. He appeared innocent and showed no signs of bad intentions.

"Look, level up. Who are you, really?" he continued.

She stared at him, wanting to believe and then lowered her eyes.

"I have a difficult time trusting anyone. I don't think I can trust you with something as important as my life."

"Are you in trouble? Is someone trying to kill you or are you on America's Most Wanted?"

Feeling cornered, she walked past him into the living room and stowed her flashlight into her bag. London tucked the gun back into its box as she sat down. She was still reluctant to reveal her identity.

He wanted her to know he would listen. She could rely on him for anything if she just believed. "If you're scared, it is the best reason to trust me."

"I'm not scared of anything or anyone. Fear isn't part of who I am."

"Clearly, I can tell. Now here is an idea, start with where you came from."

She leaned back and hesitantly began, "If you must know, I grew up in Italy. We settled in Rome when my father was sent there to work. I wanted to sing more than anything in the world, so I studied with a vocal coach, the best my father could find. I learned quickly and performed in some of the most wonderful places in Europe. I sang for diplomats and kings. It was quite a life and was on my way to becoming famous."

"What changed?"

She looked down at her hands.

"I listened in on my father's conversations. I watched him help people who were in need and I wanted to become like him. But then he was kidnapped by vigilantes and his body was never found. My mother and I are still devastated and I need justice for him."

"What does that have to do with someone trying to find you?"

"I'm not a hardened criminal, London. I'm a former FBI agent. I was undercover and framed for a crime I didn't commit. The Bureau tried me and took my badge away."

"Did they find you guilty?"

"There wasn't enough evidence. But they said I was an accomplice and had no choice but take away my privilege of service. I lost everything. No one believed me and my dad never got his justice. I worked so hard to put everything into being an agent. That was the reason I joined the force, to help individuals going through that same thing."

"How did you end up here?"

"After everything was destroyed, I had to slip away and come back to the States. My friend who worked for the Secret Service, risked his career to protect me," she looked away to hide her sadness. "It cost him his job. He knows I'm innocent. Everywhere I went I was judged as a traitor. I lost all of my friends and my life in Italy." She looked at him and refocused, "I never get paranoid, ever. But when I felt all eyes dangerously on me, I had to disappear."

She got up to walk around, feeling overwhelmed with all she had been through.

"I want to trust you, London. I just told you half of my life story. Of course, there is more. I don't know what it is, but there's something about you. It's like I'm drawn to you. Then you told me you were a detective and raised a huge red flag." Her eyes intensified and met his. "London, I need someone I can trust. I swore I would never tell anyone about myself. Besides a typical background check, I don't know anything else about you."

Her mood suddenly changed. She regretted divulging that much information and felt extremely vulnerable. So far, confiding in only one person had kept her safe.

"Maybe I shouldn't have said anything. This is a mistake!"

She got up and headed for the door. He sensed her need to run and met her. As her hand touched the knob, he blocked her exit.

Gently he affirmed, "It's okay, don't be afraid. In our line of work, we protect those who can't protect themselves. Hundreds of people have relied on you as an agent, now it's your turn. You can trust me. If this is all you have right now, then this is where you need to be."

"Agents are trained to be thick skinned and never afraid. I have been in the toughest situations on earth and seen it all. I know the men who took my father and I believe they are now after me."

"How do you know that?"

"I took something from them. They hunted me before I left, they'll do it again. Before they find me, I need more evidence. I want them put away for what they did. I want to save the only man I ever loved; my father has been everything to me." Tears filled her eyes.

London felt the pain she expressed. He had been experiencing similar emotions. It was as if they were meant to find each other. When she turned away from the door, London consoled her by putting his arm around her shoulders.

She continued, "I used to be the best at what I did for the agency. Now I'm nothing. I still haven't exposed the men who harmed my family."

"Penny, I can help you. I will keep you safe."

She shook her head, "No. I already got someone involved and endangered his life. I couldn't do that to you too."

"It's funny that we both have experience in figuring out what's between the fine lines. This case may be one of those that requires two people who are good at investigating. Maybe, I can help find these men."

"If anything leaks out, it will be the end of me and they will get away with what they are doing."

"What did you take from them?"

"I can't tell you that right now. I have ran numerous background checks and have my FBI photos. Mason Banks is someone with multiple aliases and extensive records of numerous crimes in his organization. I am still gathering evidence."

"What's your relationship with Mason?"

She looked up at his face, "I pretended to be in love with him. I disguised myself and fooled him. He made me swear not to tell anyone. He was forceful and I could sense my position was becoming more hostile. I hated being in that situation but that was what I needed to do to get the dirt on him. Soon after, he took control of me. So I took his information and got out of there. As soon as I could, I presented it to my team."

"Do you really believe your father's dead?"

"You don't know these men. They will do anything to protect their skin. Mason was threatened by my father and he's still missing."

London wanted to lessen the tension and poured himself a drink.

"You know, I did a background check on you too."

"And?"

"I found nothing. Penny Rose isn't your real name or a stage name, is it? No one with your description is out there."

"Please London, no more questions." She grabbed a notepad off of his table. "This is my way of building trust in you. Here's my number. Maybe then I will have more faith in you."

He peered over her shoulder as she wrote. When she turned, they were standing closer than expected and their eyes connected. They both felt drawn in. She instinctively leaned in, kissed his lips softly, and stepped back. When she studied his face, his eyes were sparkling.

"I thought we were the kind of friends that don't kiss," he reminded.

"We will have to make an exception for now. Tomorrow at the bar?"

"I'll be there."

On her way to her car, she was still shaky and holding back tears. It was always uncomfortable to talk about losing her father to the cruel man she was involved with. Even though she knew she was only doing her job, guilt devastated her. She had worked so hard on her own to bring Mason down. Almost everything went according to plan. She never thought she needed any man to rescue her but strangely, London was putting life back into her. She was doing the same to him.

Chapter 5

There's Something About You

The streets of downtown were quiet that night, except for the sounds of stray cats sneaking out to feast from open garbage cans in the alley. The nocturnal air was damper than usual. London sat on his bed at two in the morning, glancing out his window. As he laid back down, hand behind his head, he was holding the flyer he picked up a few weeks earlier announcing Penny Rose. He waved it back and forth, deep in thought. What was it about the woman that kept him up at night? She was obviously clever and very good at what she did.

He had his share of guesses about her past. Her exposed story appeared factual. He was beginning to think she was better at hiding than he was. What she wanted him to know was limited and might be true. He closed his eyes and vividly seen her. Every curve, every line was burnt into his brain. He knew he had to take it slow. Finding out about Penny would be a tedious process. Even though he had patience, he was being forced to wait it out. Eventually she might put enough trust in him to reveal more of herself, filling in the incomplete puzzle. Usually when someone hid out, they ran away from the problems they caused. He knew about witness protection programs. If she wasn't guilty and had something the criminal element wanted, she would have gone to her supervisor for help. Instead, her choice was to get justice without her team and government back-up. In his line of work, anyone who took the law into their own hands was asking for trouble, or a reason to get killed. She didn't seem afraid of anything, even death. He remembered reading comic books about innocent people with incredible strength and power to conquer evil. He laughingly pictured her as a super hero. From the first time he laid eyes on her, she didn't seem real. How could a beautiful woman like her have everything? No insecurities, no fear, and no one to rely on but herself. As much as he tried putting pieces together, he wasn't going to get any real answers until he built trust. In his mental investigation, he recognized she had been hurt. She said she was grieving the loss of her father, losing her career and reputation and putting a friend in jeopardy. Maybe that was where she acquired the heart of a super hero.

The question always lingered. Could she be setting him up for disaster or worse? She was obviously capable of killing if she had to. He formulated several plans and would do his best to build the trust she needed. Her body language confirmed that she wanted to confide in him.

He would go to the bar that next night to convince her to see him on a more personal level. With it being late in the hour, he had to put it to rest. He got up and rotated the blinds to block out the street light. KB jumped on the bed and curled up next to him. He couldn't help but run his hand down his back, gently petting as they fell asleep.

The next evening, after a fresh haircut, he was ready to be lulled by that mesmerizing voice. Each time he showed up, she looked his way and gave a smile. He wasn't the type to get hooked on a woman. He knew that wasn't her plan either and he didn't want to press. It was business, just business. He was determined to get what he wanted to know and he wasn't going to blow it. One false move and she would disappear, he was sure of it. Cologne and a well-fitted suit set the mood.

The bartenders recognized him and nodded his way. What started as a chance to get out of his routine now became an intrigue. A hard choice was required. Should he assist the woman or turn her in to the authorities? He would make that move when it was time.

"Hey, London, the usual?"

"Yeah. Ice this time."

"You got it."

She wasn't ready for the stage yet but looked his way. He was in his usual spot with the same drink. She stopped shying away and appeared to look forward to seeing him again. She gave a small wave as she walked over in a black satin dress. The lace hanging from her black hat, covered the upper part of her face. She tilted it enough to reveal her dazzling eyes.

"Well, I see you just can't get out of your same routine, although you did add ice to your Stoli. Will any other drastic changes be happening anytime soon?"

"It depends on the mood. I never do much more than this. Change makes me nervous."

"So this is you on a calm day?"

He grinned, "You could say that. Tell me, what else do you do outside of this environment?"

He tilted his glass waiting for an answer.

"Why do you ask?"

"Now this isn't a come on. I think the level we are on is still friendship and I don't have many friends because I keep to myself. What if I want to throw in a little change and get to know you better?"

"Didn't I already overshare with you the other night? Can't we just leave it at that?"

"We could, but why would we want to?"

"Let me think about it." She started to walk away and then turned her head, "Hey, by the way. Your cologne, it's a good touch for you."

"Thanks."

His eyes scanned the crowded room. He could understand why so many loved her entertainment. She was good. As the lights lowered, he prepared himself. As she began, he couldn't help but think Penny should be someplace better, a place where her quality of talent belonged. He could tell that she missed who she used to be. He wanted to make it his job to bring her back to the place she called home. For the moment, it was all she had. The wheels in his mind were turning. She did seem willing to build on their friendship.

When the crowds were gone and the lights opened up, she approached his table with a folded piece of paper.

London admired, "Great performance! You never cease to amaze me."

She then answered his request, "Yes, we can meet outside of the bar."

She laid a note on his table and watched him slide it into his pocket.

As she walked into the door of her home, she had a different feeling than before. Something was changing and it started to worry her. After working so hard to keep away from friends, creating friendships, and encountering lovers, she was having thoughts about London.

"Penny, how long are you going to keep singing at that place?" Joe asked with annoyance.

"Until I can find enough proof to get justice for my father."

"You should just turn yourself in and let it go to trial."

"Are you hearing yourself? You know I can't do that. Don't you remember both of us losing our jobs over this? I showed you where their operation was but we need more intel or they will just throw it out again. We both know I'm innocent."

"I know you are. I sit here thinking about the day they will find us. And then what? You need a big loophole to help you crack this case."

"I think I've found one."

"What do you mean you found one?"

"Remember the guy I met at the bar; the PI I told you about?" She threw her bag on the table and removed her shoes.

"What?! Penny, have you lost your mind? You can't trust a random guy, especially a detective."

"I really think he can help. He is kind of a recluse. He owns a cat, for crying out loud."

"That means nothing. I hope you didn't open the door to a bad decision."

"Joe, you're forgetting who I am. One of the best in the business."

"You were one of the best," he reminded.

"Don't undermine me. I am going to work this guy and have it to my advantage."

"Look at you, the confident professional," he acquiesced sarcastically.

"Joe, you kept me safe. Now it's time for me to do the same for you. Trust me. You are still the only real friend I have."

"You will be adding one more friend to the list, temporarily. Just in case, I should start searching for another place to hide when this doesn't work out."

"Don't stress it. You don't have to worry, I'll be fine."

Joe was much older than Penny and smart. He wasn't convinced that her plan would keep them out of trouble. Two people, like Penny and London rarely worked well together, especially when they were always examining each other's motives. Something about it made Joe uncomfortable, but he had to believe in her and hope that everything worked as she hoped it would.

London finished up two more cases and sent the results of his tracking to his clients. After putting her number in his phone, he texted her.

"It's London. Would you like to meet at Harbor's Edge Café today?"

She saw the message and answered right away.

"Pick me up at the bar?"

"Sounds good."

London cleared the front seat of his BMW to make room for her. He cared for his navy sedan and clothing better than his apartment. As he approached the bar, she stepped out in a pantsuit and heels. What he noticed first was her scarf and large black sunglasses.

"It's not hard to miss you dressed like that."

"I like to look classy wherever I go."

"Obviously."

"Nice car. I'm not surprised."

"Why?"

"Because you dress up at the bar." She got in and lowered her sunglasses. "It makes me wonder why your place doesn't play the same part."

He pulled out in to traffic and made a left.

"Well, that's a complicated subject," he hesitantly replied.

"It was your idea to get to know each other better. Maybe this is a good time to tell me more about yourself."

"Did anybody ever tell you have a certain persona about you?" he quizzed.

"What would that be?"

"I often refer to you as a super hero."

"Like Wonder Woman?" she chuckled.

"No, but you would be in a class right above her."

"What a compliment."

"It's just that you come off as this international spy type. Am I wrong?"

"What's wrong with playing a part that suits me?"

"Do you ever just relax? You know, in sweat pants, a pint of ice cream, watching a chick flick?"

"If the moment is right, and I wouldn't say no to a pint of ice cream."

"Okay, now were getting somewhere. You can let your hair down and be vulnerable."

"Oh no, I'm not. I'm being honest."

"Is that your strong point?"

"I think so. But there are times I have to play a role that I hate, to protect myself. You know what that's like."

"I do," he admitted.

She realized that he had reversed the conversation back to her and quickly countered, "Good job. But you never answered why your apartment is a mess and the rest of your life is not."

"Are you sure you don't want to talk about you some more? There's this mystery about you I can't quite pinpoint." he said avoiding the question.

As they were seated on the patio, she checked her surroundings and noticed that he was doing the same. She was always on high alert since training and it had become built into her.

"So, why are we here? I never interact with men I hardly know. It's out of the ordinary."

"I was intrigued by your back story. I know there is more."

"What makes you say that?"

"Experience. I noticed a sadness in your eyes and learned that you are on a mission."

"My father. I was very close to him," she sighed.

"I know that feeling."

"How so?" she returned the questioning.

"I lost my parents in an accident over two years ago."

"That explains a lot."

"Does it show that I'm still grieving?"

"A little."

He had prepared how to assure her, "Penny, I want you to know that I will never betray you. Like you, I read people very well and don't see you as a threat and I think you really need my help."

"I used to be delicate, dreaming of happiness. Everything around me was safe and loving and I never thought about seeking justice. Singing is a small way to regain that happier life until I recover innocence."

Hearing her true emotions elevated his compassion for what she had been through. He was too deeply involved to leave her alone to fend for herself.

"We can work together to get your life back."

"You? No, I couldn't put you in that place."

She felt his hand place itself on hers and sensed the sincerity in his touch. She had to admit she had not resolved her dilemma on her own.

"I am taking a big risk trusting you. My friend Joe thinks this is a bad idea. I could sink farther down that dark hole if you betray me."

He grabbed her hand, "You have my word."

She looked at him with a smile of relief. There was something beautiful inside of him that she had not experienced before.

He knew he was in too deep and couldn't walk away. He had to be part of her mission to solve what went wrong in her life. What Penny had been through and what they could face would be the most dangerous case they had ever encountered. His thoughts showed on his expression.

"What is it, London?" she asked curiously.

"I know we don't know each other very well, but from the moment I first saw you, I knew there was something there, something deep inside. When you sing, passion flows from you from behind the sadness. I might be able to figure it out in time. It just may be that we both need each other."

"I can't explain why I trust you. I still have a small fear you are going to betray me, but I want my life back."

After he dropped her off, London kept telling himself that it was only business, developing a new relationship. As a professional, he planned to stay away from anything that would make him lose focus on their objective. He was once again infused with purpose, an awakening he had not felt since he lost his parents. Somehow, he wanted to do something more for her. It wasn't to boost his morale, he sensed how desperately she needed help. He wasn't thinking about risks or what she was involved with. Even though she had not revealed all of her back story, he could see flickers of hope behind those dark eyes.

Chapter 6

Was It Worth It?

While researching one of Mason's contacts, Penny thought more about her conversation with London. She was giving in. Because her priority was to resolve her issue, it required skilled help. After all, he gave his word.

She opened one of the boxes stacked against the wall and examined her certificates of excellence during training and after. She proved good at what she was trained for but had still not exacted justice for her father. She hadn't talked to her mother in a while and wondered if it would be a good time to check in. She studied her family pictures, reliving memories of better times before her father, Andrew, was apprehended by the men she hated. She held in her other hand the one thing those men feared, evidence that held the key to setting her free. She had captured emails, text messages and a microchip with their plans. Revenge dominated her. It was imperative to incriminate those who took what belonged to her and wreaked havoc on her family.

So why hadn't anyone believed her? They said it was because she was involved in their crimes. She had participated in their deceit and became just like them. Transforming herself to get in had backfired. After she was caught, Mason and his men were nowhere to be found. She was left alone with guilt and apparent testimony that she was part of their operation. Her disguise worked too well. When she presented her own evidence, the Bureau said the video footage was contrived to make her appear innocent. They viewed other videos connected with one of Mason's men who turned himself in. His story was that she was not only heavily involved but leading operations. When she was asked to turn over all the documents, she held back some that were important to her personally. The small amount of what the Feds used was not enough for a conviction. Her superiors agreed that it was best to let her go on her own recognizance, without a future position in the Bureau again. They took her badge, dismissed her, and ended her career. She saved the newspaper clipping of her trial and pictures that defamed her career. They were short but sad. That was the day she lost everything she had built.

Putting her memories back in their box, she began to think how she and London might make a good team. A dynamic duo solving her case.

With all the nostalgia she was experiencing, she decided to call her mother. They hadn't talked since the incident to protect her from danger. Using her computer, she patched through a few networks that would give her a minute of an untraceable call.

"Penny, I'm so happy you finally called. Where are you?" Evelyn quickly asked.

"I can't tell you where I am right now. I'm so tired of running. I'm working with a professional investigator."

"I think about you every day, wondering if you are safe. I understand why you don't call but when will you end this charade and be yourself again?"

"I'm sorry for all the trouble. I am singing again."

"You always had that passion in your voice. I just want you to come home, honey. We can sort all the details and get you help. When we couldn't solve what happened to your father, it devastated both of us. I let it go and so should you."

"I can't, Mom. My name has been smeared and my life is in jeopardy. I need to get it back to where it was."

"I know you're innocent and you want justice. What makes you think this person can help free you of your misery?"

"I have to trust him. Joe helps too and keeps me safe. I know it looked like I was involved with Mason, but I have proof that he was the one who killed my father."

"I have never found closure with his death because they never did find him. Somehow, I believe he might be alive somewhere."

"I would love to believe that. I have been thinking about you and how much I want us together soon. I want to come back to Italy."

"We've had wonderful memories here. Your father was your biggest fan." Evelyn broke down.

"Mom, please don't cry. I'm going to make sure we get it all back."

"I'm not so sure. When you started this, you looked so different and then you changed everything about yourself."

"If you understand, then you will be patient and let me finish this."

"I realize that. I miss you, darling."

"I know. We'll be together soon, I promise."

Evelyn could do nothing but trust her daughter to keep her word. The distance was getting to her. From the day Penny started working for the FBI, her mother knew there was danger that only increased pursuing those men. Evelyn was missing Andrew and did not want to move on as a widow.

She understood why her daughter rarely called and kept a low profile, but her thoughts tossed through her mind like a torrential ocean storm with waves crashing against the rocks. After her husband and daughter disappeared, nothing was calm. Life had changed abruptly and she awaited solace to reappear. That day, one phone conversation was enough to help her through her week. Evelyn had heard the voice of her daughter. That was what she needed to give her strength, knowing both women could recover their lives. As she hung up the phone, Evelyn looked over at the photo of her husband holding their only child. Could Penny, on her own, rescue her and ease her mind? It was all she had left for hope. Evelyn was alone with only memories to make her smile. She trusted Penny to come up with a plan to bring life back to normal.

With the help of a man holding her trust and confidence, Penny would push as far as she could.

She would risk her life and the lives of those who helped her. Emotionally tired of running and hiding, she was growing weaker in her strategizing. Why did she have that feeling about London when she saw him at the bar that day? What was it about him that made her break the oath to trust no one? Her instincts may have been correct, but she found it necessary to continually test the waters. She was still on high alert for warning signs of lies or betrayal and reminded herself that it was still the best choice to push forward in her personal investigation.

London had no idea what he was getting involved in. The life of Penny Rose was littered with complications that were beyond the norm. He had never been involved with anyone from the Secret Service or the FBI. It was deeper and more treacherous than anything he experienced on the force. The man could not see his future but did feel himself alive again. Suddenly, his skills were useful and exciting. He stopped considering getting out of the business. Even though they spent very little time socializing in public, he could see the desperation in her brown eyes. Her mission was of great importance.

For London, things around him took on a different appearance. Weeks before, he was depressed, surrounded by loss, and felt sorry for himself. He stood in his kitchen and looked around his apartment, realizing what his depression did to his life and his home. He had to do something about it. It would take a few days to clean up. With the help of a service, the place would get its proper deep cleaning. Magazines and newspapers went into the recycle bin. He threw out some clothes, shredded old files, and organized his desk. Two cans of white paint and some elbow grease gave his rooms a refresh. He donated his old couch and ordered a new one along with a thick area rug, something he never owned before. Planning to spend time researching with Penny, he thought about calling in food service delivery. Meal kits would save time shopping for groceries.

Penny Rose had influenced him, making him a better man. His was a cold and uncaring business and his clients made him feel used. The thrill of the hunt was rewarded by releasing and moving on to the next person with another familiar story. With Penny, it was very personal. He couldn't quite grasp everything but his reward was saving her life. Conversely, she was indirectly doing the same for him. Together, they could accomplish great things for each other. The motivation gave him courage to begin to change his life to his own.

Recently, his apartment felt renewed and even London himself had become unrecognizable. He was grasping a meaning in his life by helping a fellow human that he cared about. It was what he had been reaching for since his parents death. Even though he was changing, he still couldn't bring himself to walk into his parents' home. Instead, he would lift their picture and talk to himself, staring at what used to be.

"Oh, Dad, what should I do? How can I go on without your wisdom? You devoted your love to me. A part of me doesn't want to move on. Is it wrong to feel this way?"

Those thoughts often reappeared at night. He wondered if Penny Rose had the same feelings after losing her father. He refused to believe in fate or the force that was bringing them together. But if two people needed each other, why did the light only shine on them when they met? He had never felt that before. It was confusing and amazing. His mind drifted. What was she doing that very minute? Was she dreaming or plotting? Was it revenge and anger lurking behind her beauty and sultry tones that lulled men to their knees? He wondered what other disguises she used. It was obvious that she could get into the criminal mind. She was good at putting on an act to clean up their mess while they caused pain and suffering. Like him, she was obsessed with the hunt. Of course, he knew that the name she went by was not hers. He wasn't stupid. He liked to think he was smarter than most investigators in the city. Like Penny, he taught himself how to read those who were lying and concealing things. But for her, he was knowingly leaving himself open to her; a risk he was willing to take. For the night, he had nothing more to go on or research. He would wait for her to reveal more of herself when she was ready.

The next morning, Penny showed up at his apartment to release her worry. Deciding not to burden Joe with her troubles, she slipped out before he awoke. It felt odd to her that she trusted London more and in a way she had never experienced before.

"I hope I'm not imposing. I just need to talk," she pleaded quietly.

"No, it's fine. Come on in."

She studied the room and noticed the changes. It smelled better, looked orderly, and even the cat seemed happier.

"Wow, I love what you've done with the place. What gave you the motivation?" she asked.

"I think I just needed a reason to get out of what wasn't letting the light in."

"What's the reason?"

"You. I mean, helping you gave me the drive to improve. Believe it or not, I used to be highly organized and clean."

"I'm flattered by your reason. Thank you, but I'm not that special."

"I think you are. You have no idea what you have done for me."

"I never thought I would have that kind of an impact on anyone. I'm glad you're impressed by me."

London wondered what was going on in her head. He took her seriously, but charging into the unknown with her kind of trouble was a bit frightening, even though he had been in scary situations before.

He opened the subject, "I want to think about the bigger picture. What we are taking on is risky, but necessary to redeem yourself. I want to be one-hundred percent part of it."

"I appreciate that."

Something was different. Penny was not wearing her usual makeup and her hair was in a soft bun with strands resting alongside her face. She was no less attractive without the glamour. He noticed that she looked cold and needed comfort. He retrieved a warm blanket from his bedroom and wrapped her in it. Penny took off her shoes and sat on the couch next to him.

"Can I get you anything else?" he asked.

"No. This is fine." Her expression was melancholy.

"Where are you right now?" London asked.

"In my head, I guess. I have been working on this alone and now, for the first time, I'm going to get justice with help. That makes me nervous, you know?"

"Yeah, I get it. You're saying you're scared for the first time."

"Is that what I'm feeling, fear?"

"It seems like it. You don't have anything to fear with me. I really want to work with you."

"What makes you think that this time it can be done?"

"Entering into the unknown always feels intimidating. I've been there myself, but I have faith in you."

She looked away and put her forefinger near her lips and said nothing. He watched her breathing as she gazed distantly. Penny wanted to say what she was thinking but decided to keep it to herself.

"Penny, you have thoughts I would love to explore."

"I'm not sure I want to be that vulnerable."

"Tell me what you're feeling."

"I talked to my mother today."

"You don't sound happy. Shouldn't that be good?"

"Well, yes. I haven't talked to her in a long while."

"I take it she is aware of your situation."

"Yes. I can't tell her everything, but I want her safe. That is all I care about. I don't think they are interested in coming after her. It's me they want."

"What makes you so sure they are still looking for you?"

"When I was in their quarters, before I was caught, I took pictures of documents that could lead me to my father. They had underground operations with numerous people working for them. Most of it was encrypted. It was hard to say whether all of those people knew exactly how corrupt Mason was, nonetheless, they were involved. They know I have confidential information about them."

"Why haven't they found you by now?"

"They are probably still looking, but we have taken great efforts to conceal ourselves. I received my first warning from them while I was still at the Bureau."

"What was it?"

"We haven't forgotten our revenge."

"I'm not trying to minimize your feelings, but I used to get threatening letters from people who didn't want to get caught. It bothered me. I guess we try to be tough inside, but the fact of the matter is, we are all human," he explained supportively.

"It isn't because I am a woman?"

"That has nothing to do with it. Have you ever been in a situation where you felt trapped in your line of work?"

"Yes. We were on a mission that took the lives of two of my fellow agents. They were in the line of fire and I had to rescue the ones who made it out alive. Afterwards, I broke down and cried, trying to pull it together. I always wish there was more I could have done. I still gave way to tears."

"Human, that's what you were. In that moment, you displayed empathy for the lost souls."

She took a breath and sat straighter, "I'm not afraid to take these men down, London. What I am afraid of is that other lives will be taken because of me."

"You had nothing to do with what happened to those who died. You did your job. Those you saved were grateful for your sacrifice."

"Now I have to try and confront what I lost. What if nothing good comes out of this?"

"Investigators tend to doubt whether we are worthy enough to take on the bigger tasks. I've had my share of threats and bad things happen. I was never the type to yell and threaten to get the truth, but I have had to pressure those I questioned and there were times I went home and couldn't sleep from anxiety. Then I would have to refocus on why I do it. What is your big why?"

"I miss my mother. I can't see her or be with her until this is finished."

He admitted that he missed his mother too. She looked at him and forced a smile while putting her feet under the blanket.

"I believe in you. So, tell me, why do you think those men took your father?"

"They operate a business outside of the law. I was in the States when I learned he vanished."

"Is this what made you want to be an agent?"

"No. It was before that. I was here with the Bureau at the time and not in Italy."

"So the authorities in Italy went to find him?"

"They searched for weeks and never found him. So, I went after them. I wanted to rescue him who couldn't help himself. According to the FBI, I crossed a line and wasn't supposed to take the case on my own. It was too dangerous or something like that. They were never completely clear about it. I had to do it myself and put myself in harm's way. Security cameras and guards surrounded their headquarters, making it difficult to get in or get information. For years we thought Mason was a good man. He had been my father's friend since we arrived in Rome. It looked like my father approached him and threatened to expose him. Losing his committed friendship, Mason felt betrayed. Even though my father had no authority to arrest him, he wanted to stop him. He knew he was responsible because *'The paper trail doesn't lie',* my father would say."

"With all the evidence you have, why couldn't they stop him?"

She sighed, "It wasn't enough to pin it on Mason. From their view, it was a bunch of petty offenders that came and went with nobody in charge. Except for the guy who said I was in charge."

"And when you infiltrated, did you procure enough evidence to prove otherwise?

"Not according to them. They claimed it was me running it, that I was an integral part of the gang! All their evidence implicated me, but I swear that it wasn't. I have all of the names to show who are actively involved. Of course, it is coded, making it hard for me figure who is who."

"So, what do we do now?"

"I thought about it and I'm not telling Joe about the details you and I are working on. He knows about you. Let me start by showing you the documents and photographs and the saved newspaper archives to bring you up to speed." She paused for a minute and he waited, listening.

"London, you realize I'm putting everything into this. Joe is furious that I am even working with you. He has been there for me all this time, like a father, and I don't want him to think I no longer care about him."

Because it sounded like she was protecting him from something, he asked, "What is he to you?"

"Are you assuming he's a good looking spy who dreams to sweep me off my feet?"

"No, well, yes. He sounds like a secret spy."

"He's not a spy. He's much older than me, way over fifty. He was great at what he did. He protected several presidents and congressmen. He once took a bullet for someone very important."

"Who was it?"

"I don't know. He can't tell me that. He did show me the scar. He said the bullet fragments are still in his flesh."

"What made you put your life in his hands?"

"He reminded me of my father. When things became life-threatening, he knew what to do and how to do it. We came together and he gave up everything for me. He is good at security but not at investigating."

"Has he ever been married?"

"No. Like me, he was devoted to his job."

"I'm sorry he lost what he loved to do."

"So am I. It took me a while to get over the guilt when he used everything he had to protect me. So, him knowing that I trust you, scares him."

He took in everything she told him about her history. Where they had to go from there was going to be complex and dangerous. She continued to relate how she wanted to proceed, never realizing that even if she got justice, her life might never be the same.

After outlining the objectives and plans that had not worked and others that might, she stopped speaking. He let the silence fill the room. London had no words to add as he pondered each byte of information slowly. Just then, she leaned and put her head on his shoulder. His arm naturally went around her, keeping her warm. He felt that she needed to be comforted and held by someone. As she inched closer, she looked up at him and he pulled the hair from her face, touching her cheek.

"Do you really want to live your life as a nomad if this doesn't work out?" he wondered.

"I have to. It's my only way."

Just then, he gently kissed her lips. She did not immediately pull away. When she gently pushed herself back, he stared at her.

"Why did you do that?" she asked quietly.

"I thought you wanted me to."

"No, I can't be kissed by you."

"I'm sorry. I didn't plan it."

"I know, it's not you. I can't let myself get this close."

"I never want to make you feel uncomfortable. It won't happen again."

"You wouldn't want to be with someone like me. When this is over, I'll be on my way. I guess you could say I'm a rolling stone."

"I just looked into those weepy eyes and seen how much you need saving."

"I don't need saving. I need to be free."

Her eyes spoke what she could not say. He could see what she was feeling. She just wanted to feel safe while being held without saying a word.

After a few minutes together, she started to think and get in her head. Getting off the couch, she walked over and grabbed her keys and coat. As Penny bent down to put on her shoes, London put his hands behind his head and sighed deeply. He didn't want to think that he crossed the line. He had to remember that her position was stressful with serious consequences. She straightened up, touched his face and turned for the door. London thought of the promise he made to himself that he would be there for her.

"When do we get together to finish this?" he asked.

"Tomorrow. Come to the bar tonight and hear me sing. I will feel better if you are there. Let's pretend it is just you and I, no one else."

"I'll be there."

She walked out without looking back. Being free was more important than falling for a man who could quite possibly be the one for her, a devoted hero and savior. The real truth was that he couldn't get her out of his head or heart. He feared her redemption would take her away from him. Was that worth it? What was it all for? Justice, punishment, to clear her name? He came to the conclusion that she could never give herself to him.

She had walked a fine line with the FBI and broke her promise. He could see that she was tired of her adjusted life. If they asked, would she go back to the Bureau? He was sure she had thought about it often. Even though she was playing it tough, inside she was an emotional woman who wanted to lose the ache. London hoped to take the pain away and ease her fears. It would become the most challenging case of his life.

\

Chapter 7

Reveal Yourself to Me

Sully was asked to train new recruits at the local broadcasting station. The younger generation admired and trusted him as a reporting mentor. They always reached for the popular dream to present the national evening news. As he was leaving the station, his cell phone rang. It was London.

"Lon. Perfect timing. I just finished training the new anchors."

"They're being trained by the best."

"I can see you are biased."

"Yes, I am."

"What's your reason for calling?" Sully got to the point.

"I wanted to let you know I'm feeling better. I made a few changes and taking on a new case."

"Your voice sounds confident. What's the case about?"

"I can't tell you much about it. I'm helping a friend, so I may not be around when you want to reach me. I'm going to FBI Headquarters."

"FBI? London, what are you involved with?"

Sully was worried. He thought of London as a son.

"When the time is right, I will let you in on it. For now, I have to abide by the strictest of confidence. You will be happy to know that I fixed up my apartment."

"Are you still keeping the cat's name?" He was making light of the conversation.

"Yes; KB is better than calling him Keyboard."

"Oh yes, much better." He paused, "London, be careful. Working around the Feds, well, that's a different kind of investigation."

"I know. I have to do it this way. I need to help this person."

"This person wouldn't happen to be a woman?"

"Goodbye, Sully." He put a little melody to his words.

"Keep in touch, Lon."

London knew Penny's plan to go to the Bureau after obtaining enough information. For the time, she was not revealing her real name to him. There were some secrets she needed to keep to herself...until later.

Joe had been out for the day, giving her the time to collect her files. She carefully searched and omitted anything containing her real name and slid it into a small backpack. Business discussions were always at London's place, to avoid a trace. She would share her files in detail and fill him in as much as she could. When she arrived, London could see the concern on her face.

"Are you sure you want to do this?" he asked.

"Yes. I gathered what I could for you to see into my world. Are you having second thoughts? I would think since you are an investigator you would have some confidence."

"Well, there is always a little nervousness when you are finding the truth about someone. I was only thinking about your safety."

"Don't worry about me. This is all about my father. I forgot about myself when he disappeared. I'm very sure I want to do this."

She took out a picture of her father and mother. She wanted him to see where her motivation came from.

"Your father was very handsome for his age," London observed.

"He was. Mother and I loved him very much. I noticed a picture of your parents. You have the same sad ache as I do."

"Yeah, and the same pain. My friend wants me to leave this apartment and move into my parents place."

"Is it yours?" she asked.

"Yes. They left it to me in their will. I haven't been able to go inside since the accident."

She could see there was a quiet pain and struggle in his face just getting the words out. It was another reason she wanted him to assist her through it all. He caught himself and refocused.

"Are those your documents?" he pointed.

"What I have are some of the pictures I took and copies of the files I found."

"What kind of operation are they into?"

"Fake passports and visas. They give criminals access in and out of the country. When my father found out about it, he tried to pin Mason down."

"What is your dad's history with him?"

"He was an old friend. When my father became a Consul, Mason was working alongside the Ambassador. He was a good man at one time. They spent a lot of time together with others in their business, wine tasting, dinner parties, and socializing. Mason was a trusted man in his circle."

"Let me guess, he started his own espionage service."

"Yes. He was going through the files, searching out easy targets. He hired men to make fake passports, visas and other documents and it became lucrative. When that wasn't enough, he had these young kids, teenagers, stealing purses and backpacks from tourists. They could have kept the money, but Mason wanted the IDs. They would turn them over to Mason and then he would use it and sell it."

"And how was your father involved?"

"He confronted Mason, and he denied it. They had too little evidence to convict him, so they let him go. After he was fired, he became very hostile towards my father."

"Where is Mason now?"

She pulled out a flash drive. "This shows where their operations used to be."

They loaded it into his computer and scanned through it. Penny pointed out how their operation was with access to the back street and how Mason preferred an office with a direct route to his henchmen.

While still an FBI agent, she had pitched the idea to her supervisors to go after Mason. They assumed she was an angry daughter wanting vengeance and dismissed her idea. She was willing to go incognito and use her wiles to persuade their dark organization. She wanted them to believe and trust her. There was nothing to convince the FBI to take on the case and they told her that it was not hers to play with. If there was something to find, other agents would take on the task without her involvement. She knew she was meant to do it.

Once she worked her way in, she cut off communication with the agency. During her time with Mason, he had no idea she was Andrew's daughter. She walked the halls like a professional actress deserving an Academy Award. No one suspected a thing. Mason hadn't seen past her disguise, playing a role to get information. He enjoyed her natural beauty and used every way to gain control of her. She would use her skills to steal for him instead of hiring useless young boys to steal petty amounts. He gave her anything she asked. She was ashamed of what she was doing and not working with the Bureau made her feel worse.

What they wouldn't do to rectify it, she would have to do on her own.

When she finally left and released her evidence to prove her suspicions, the Feds were furious. Acting on her own had left a bitter note. They used to trust her. What was the reason they suddenly did not? They discriminated against her by letting it sit until they felt like pursuing Mason and his group. When they finally raided the operation, the gang had already moved out, leaving Penny alone with the blame. The man keeping watch behind the building was taken into custody and would only point fingers at Penny. The building contained nothing. All that was left was the evidence Penny acquired and an unresolved case. Her defeat had led to sharing it with a PI in a small apartment.

London interrupted his perusal, "All of this seems legit. There is more here than you originally turned over, especially that list of names. I think we could take this to the Bureau again."

"That's my plan. I want to face them and come out of hiding."

"How long until you can do that?"

"I don't know. I don't feel it yet."

"Your hesitation is real."

"After they left the place where Mason was, I asked around. Someone gave me information about where they moved to. I promised to protect their identity if they helped. That was when I was told that they were the ones who kidnapped my father."

"That was brave. Did you go check it out?"

"I did. I was careful not to be seen. I hid and took pictures of Mason walking out of his building with two other men, wearing Armani suits and expensive shoes. Once, they had a man with his hands tied behind his back and a piece of cloth around his head. I could swear it was my father."

"Then what?"

"I followed them. They threw the man to the ground and three men beat him and put him in the trunk of another car. It was painful to watch but I recorded it."

"Were you still with the Bureau when this happened?"

"No. It was right after they fired me and I decided to take it on my own. I panicked, thinking that man could be my father. When the Feds saw me reach out to Joe for help, they warned him to stay away from me. When I begged Joe to help me and showed him my evidence, he could see my life was threatened. He offered his protection and was fired for having anything to do with me. He was brave enough to sacrifice everything. When both of us went to Mason's, his men saw us and fired shots. Joe and I managed to get away safely. Then he worked out a plan to change everything and leave without a trace. Because he was originally from California, he knew of a good place to hide. We've been here for a couple of months and know it won't be long until they locate us."

"And then you fell back on what you really loved, singing. Will you continue to sing after your victory? A strong woman like yourself deserves to conquer all the evil you've been through."

She exhaled as she pondered, "Somehow I want to believe he is still alive. I've known Mason to kill men for betraying him. The guy who was caught was glad he went to jail because he would have ended up dead if he stayed with him. But he kept saying that I was involved in all of it."

"Someday we can lay that to rest."

As he continued examining her papers and photos, he didn't completely understand why the FBI refused to accept her story. He wasn't an attorney, but it all seemed believable and enough to release her. Penny told him how she appreciated the way he organized her case and used deductive reasoning to clear her from guilt. London studied her face after stacking the papers back in her bag. He could see she was overwhelmed living a recurring nightmare. It had been long overdue to see Mason get what was coming to him.

"No, it's okay. I can handle it," she said quietly to herself.

"This has to be the hardest thing you ever do in the name of your father. Revealing yourself brings me to my own knees experiencing your pain."

"I want to be strong again. I want it so badly. I will get them to believe me. I will risk it all or die trying!"

He brought his chair closer and came to her side. Wanting to be supportive, his arm wrapped around her. Her desperation was evident and he would follow and listen to what she needed. She knew the FBI better than he did and he believed her story. Could it be that they just didn't like her? She was going to confront them about their accusations and explain her case. Someone would have to listen.

Listen or not, she was still going to go through with it and then retrieve new information about Andrew.

"Well, do we have enough to go on before we leave?" he asked.

"I think so. I hope you're ready for this. It may be the ride of your life."

"Oh, I truly believe you on that one."

He thought about her gig at The Red Fedora and asked, "What are you going to do about your job at the bar?"

"I told Steven that I have to be out of town. He said Sasha can play piano until I get back."

"You have hopes of returning?"

"I don't know what the future holds for me. For now, I would like to think I have a future somewhere. I want to keep all of the options open."

"To me, you are resilient. You will always find your calling. Solving crimes with you, well, that's another story."

"A super hero persona, perhaps?" she retorted.

He couldn't help but smile at her comment.

Lifting her bag over her shoulder, she turned her eyes toward him, "Beats following cheating spouses and liars, right?"

"We'll see about that. I may have to return to that life someday."

"I promise you, you won't. Follow my lead, stay by me, and listen to everything I tell you. Don't lean on your own skills. Trust me to keep you safe and if you listen, you will stay alive."

"Why is it so appealing when a woman takes charge?"

"Don't be fooled. I think with my head and then my strength. I can still beat you down if I have to," she joked.

"Ever since I met you, I knew that as a fact."

She wasn't sure what she would tell Joe about her trip. She hadn't left California since they arrived. Maybe she wouldn't say anything. Regardless of what he thought, she would do what she must. She booked a flight for the two of them, setting the scene for their next move.

In her room, she was going through her things and packing a bag. Joe looked in, wondering what she was doing.

"What's going on?" he asked shocked.

"Going on a trip." She didn't look at him as she continued to arrange personal items between her clothes.

"What do you mean you are going on a trip? You know that's just inviting danger."

He looked at the files lying on her bed and his emotions took over. His voice showed authority mixed with fear.

"Those are the files! From the looks of it, you are determined to get what you want. I hope you don't go about it like you did last time!"

"Yes, I am going after Mason again."

"We agreed that you would not leave California. Those men are ruthless and you are entering into a high-risk. It's foolishness! They will kill you for sure and I won't be there to get you out this time."

"Joe, if I don't do this, the both of us will never get a normal life. Hiding out for the rest of your life, you really want that?!"

He took a breath and recomposed, "Penny, I think of you as a daughter, you know that. My time with the Secret Service is over. With my age and experiences, I am done. But as for you, I know how important this is to you. As much as we tried to hide it, I am an accomplice."

She stopped and put her hand on his arm.

"I know this is my fault and I want what is best for you and me. This is not a selfish effort. I have a father and mother to think about. I appreciate that you want me safe, but I have to do this."

He wasn't comfortable listening to her reasoning. She was young and beautiful and it wasn't fair to keep her locked away in misery, watching her grieve over her beloved father. Joe knew he was different. He could sit it out and wait patiently for the right time. Putting off anything was not her style. She could act as a soft spoken singer with natural talent, but in reality, she had always been determined to change the wrong. Her life had been captured and she had to work relentlessly to get back what was hers.

"I want to say how stupid you are, but I can't. I guess there is nothing I can do to stop you. I hope you fight hard to get what you want."

"Respectfully, I appreciate that you want to protect me from distress, but this is right. I thank you for everything, including letting me do this."

He observed her face to see that she was prepared for what was to come.

"Are you going alone?"

He knew her answer.

"No. I'm taking London."

"Are you falling for this man?"

"No. He knows the business and how to help me. Trust me, Joe, when I get my life back, you will be the first to know and the both of us can finally be free."

He nodded, "I hope so."

"You know my history. We have both been in dangerous situations and are trained to stay alive. I will be fine."

"There isn't anyone with the strength and drive like you. Just be careful."

"I will."

As he gave her a gentle hug, his heart was broken. She was the only family he had and the last thing he wanted to lose. He had been carrying her sadness with him and gave her the love he thought a daughter needed. Their friendship strengthened her resolve.

As her taxi driver pulled up to the white loading zone, her door opened and she stepped out, beautifying the grey concrete with elegance. She stood out. Travelers and attendants couldn't help but notice her gait. Her stunning dress moved gracefully like something out of a 1950's movie; deep, dark red with a hat to match. Elegance and class was an intrinsic part of her style. London arrived earlier and was standing just inside the terminal when she appeared. His smile was obvious as he watched.

"You are a woman who packs light. I expected to see about six bags with you," he greeted.

"I'm not like every other woman out here. Style means a lot but we have real business to attend to."

"I love that you are not like anyone out here. Penny Rose, the woman who lives on the edge of grace and danger."

"That is who I have become."

After they finally boarded, she lifted her carry-on.

"Here, I can do that for you," he offered.

"We talked about this. Do you really think I need a man to come to my rescue and help with my bags?" He knew her question was meant to be comical.

"I'm sorry. I keep forgetting who you are. Many apologies to you, Miss Penny."

"You know I take care of myself. I'm not used to being carried along, needing someone to lend a hand."

Once in the air, they scanned the cabin again evaluating passengers, just in case. Settled in, she crossed her legs and sipped her drink, peering out the window. She was pondering what it would be like when it was over. What would life be like going back with her mother and knowing Joe was living an easier life without worry? And London? She could not allow him to get in harm's way. She would make sure of that. Even though she told herself that she was not in love, she experienced strong feelings with him. She had to confess that he made a good friend and his sincerity was welcomed. It felt good to trust someone and feel their care.

No matter how long it might take, she believed she would be rewarded for what she risked. It might not be perfect and it would take effort, but she didn't care about the level of difficulty. She had trained for it. She wanted it to happen her way.

Descending into Washington, D.C. brought back strong memories of her career. She had worked at the main headquarters near the town where her father was born and raised. With her resume, she received high rankings on her missions and was well respected. The sound of London's voice broke her thoughts.

"I'm impressed by what you had to achieve to work here. I heard only one in five are accepted."

"It was my first choice. I was fortunate they chose me."

Inside the hotel, the bellboy brought their bags to their rooms. London's was next door. She washed her hands and freshened up, checking her makeup and hair. She unpacked her things, including the documents, and laid them on the bed when she heard the door.

"It's London."

"I was just unpacking. How's your room?" she asked.

"It's nice. Better than a cheap motel."

"Be sure not to use the open bar. They are so overpriced," she said looking around her room.

"I think I knew that. But thanks for your concern."

"I noticed they have a restaurant and bar downstairs. We can go there later," she said as she entered the bathroom.

She shut the door briefly and London continued to look around while waiting. His eyes scanned the documents on the bed. With a quick glance at the bathroom door, he picked up the passport. Simone Harlow. Hearing the door, he quickly put it back and walked to the other side as she came out.

"I need to relax. Do you want to do something before we go to headquarters tomorrow?"

"What do you have in mind?"

'They have a pool here. I haven't had a swim since I left Italy."

"I'd like that. When would you like to go?"

"We could go now. I just removed my makeup."

London could see that she possessed a genuine beauty. He loved looking at her without makeup and had to tell himself to stop staring.

He met her poolside and noticed her attractive form. The swimsuit flattered her shape. Sitting at the edge of the pool, her feet were floating in the water and she leaned back when she saw him.

"I thought you would have been in the water by now," he mentioned.

"I was waiting for you. You clean up nice without the suit."

"I don't do a lot of swimming. We used to swim when I was in college when they had frat parties."

He sat next to her.

"It feels good."

"I need to do more things like this," she admitted.

"Chasing bad guys from a hotel room?"

"No, silly. Relaxing. Appreciating life more than I do. I don't take very good care of myself," she said.

"From where I'm sitting, it's evident you do."

"I'm being serious."

"Okay, what do you want to do?"

"I want to travel around the world. I want to take care of my mom and live out my years being happy."

"Who says you can't do that?"

"I don't know what the future holds for me."

"Let me tell you what it will be like," he coaxed.

"No one can predict the future. But okay, you give it your best shot."

"I see you having a good life. Your voice will be heard by thousands who adore you. You will always have a smile and it will reflect onto those you touch with your song."

"What else do you see?"

"I see you having a family and committing yourself to one man for the rest of your life."

"That's a nice vision but I don't see it the way you do."

"I think you should see it optimistically. It makes the goal easier to achieve."

"You would think. For me, I just see it all alone, without anyone to share it with."

"Could you ever see it with me?"

She quickly got up and dove into the deep end. When she emerged, she pulled her hair back and swam closer.

"So you don't have an answer for me?" he asked.

"I can't answer a question like that. It's too soon to think about you and I being together that way."

He smiled and respected her comment. He was going to enjoy his time with her and not complicate anything further. He didn't want her stressed. He jumped in and began swimming too.

They spent a little time in the pool and then soaked in the hot tub. She suggested how she could use a good meal and some wine. He was up for the idea, so they grabbed their towels and dried off before going to their rooms. As London stepped into the bathroom for a shower, he thought about what he found in her room. Sitting at the pool with her, he tried to think of her as Penny Rose, but in her face he saw Simone. How would she feel if she knew he was snooping through her things? He was feeling a little guilty and thought about confessing. He wanted nothing to stand behind her new found trust. For the night, he should probably keep it secret.

The time came when they entered the Bureau. She was nervously optimistic, prepared, and ready to look them in the eye to demand they hear her out. She approached the reception desk and asked for the head supervisor.

"Can I help you?"

"I'd like to speak to Kenneth Boroughs."

"Is he expecting you?"

"No. Is he in?"

"What is the nature of your visit?"

Just as Penny was about to answer, a man who was near overheard her. Jarod Fisher worked alongside Penny for a few years. He was a good friend and became immediately curious why she had returned.

"Excuse me. I'll take care of them," Jarod spoke up. "What are you doing here?"

Seeing Jarod brought back memories of better times together. It was good to see a familiar face from her past. She had to think of her mission and it was not the time for a happy greeting.

"Jarod, I want to see Kenneth."

"You know he won't see you. You got thrown off the force when they found out about you."

"I know, I was there." She wanted to use force in her voice, but held back, trying to remain calm and professional.

He motioned, "Let's talk in the public conference room over here."

He led them to a private room adjoining the lobby, hoping no one would spot them right away. He knew that he would be in trouble if he was seen with her. He had known about the case. When they worked together, he mentioned that he was on her side. He wasn't a superior, but he knew more about what was going on than most. Jarod helping her was something she was half expecting.

"Now, why are you here?" Jarod asked abruptly as he looked around. He was watchful and cautious, and always faced the door. He watched warily, not wanting anyone to observe them.

"I have information about Mason and what he did to my father. You know I'm innocent."

He kept his voice low, "We went through all of that. They said your case was weak and found you were part of an operation you had no business in."

"Jarod, I have the proof now. Mason set me up to look like I was guilty. Even though I wasn't supposed to take the assignment on my own, I found admissible evidence. He is guilty on several counts."

"You may have proof, but the case was closed. What are you planning on doing? Nothing stupid, I hope."

"We worked hard organizing this. I need to show Kenneth these docs and then the force can catch Mason. I may be the only one who knows about it."

Just then, they heard the door knob turn and open. Kenneth was a tall man full of authority and was clearly disturbed by her presence.

"What are you doing here?! I thought we would never see your face again after we threw you out," he blurted.

"Good to see you too, Kenneth. Do you really think I came here to make trouble? I have been hiding out from Mason and now I am the only person who can put him away."

"You're not welcomed here. It won't bring back your father. Who knows why they kidnapped him? Maybe he was as involved as you were." His sarcastic tone showed his anger was ready to burst.

"You want me out of the way, don't you?! I want to be free of the prison you put me in. I'm here to prove my innocence."

"That's why we fired you. And for you to come in here, thinking it's okay to grill Jarod on a closed case you have no business in, puts you in a bad place. You put yourself in that prison. We did the research and we found nothing. I suggest you leave immediately before I have you removed."

"I think you better do what he says," Jarod quietly agreed.

Kenneth's rage caused him to gush further, "You were a sensible woman. You wanted something and you went after it. But this time you did it the wrong way, your way! You have wasted your time coming here because we have nothing for you; a sly traitor who got away. There is nothing more you can do. But if I had my way, you'd be in prison by now."

She stepped up to him, "You listen to me. I will find these men and when I do, I will rub it in your face! It was wrong to fire me and you know it. I had no other choice but to try and save my father. I will find a way to get justice for him somehow."

"Your father is probably dead and it's all your fault. You took it upon yourself to break the law." He looked at London, "Is this man part of your resentful scheme?"

"Hey, don't talk to her like that!" London spoke up.

The room got quiet and all eyes went to her. Jarod opened the door.

"You have no business being here, either of you. Leave now!" Kenneth demanded, pointing his finger towards the exit.

He watched them leave for the lobby, then turned and stormed away in disgust.

As Penny passed Jarod, he slid a note into her hand.

"My cell. Call me tonight. Something you should know." he whispered.

As they descended the steps outside, London walked beside her, thinking about what had just happened.

"Well, that didn't go like I planned," she said surprised.

"He's not a very nice man."

"He never was."

"Where do we go from here?"

"I am talking to Jarod tonight. I'm not sure what's going to happen. Something is just not right with Kenneth."

"I didn't like what he said about you being responsible for your father missing."

"I know it's not true. He was just trying to break me and make me give up. I won't let that happen."

"I can see that you don't let anyone push you around. You really stood up to him."

"No one stands in my way."

As they waited for a cab, he added a question.

"Are there any other surprises you want to share with me?"

"No. You seem to know everything about me now. I've never been married, I have no battle scars, and I can be stubborn. That's it. Anything else you need to know?"

"There's always something."

"I'm still me, so don't get any ideas about changing me into some super hero, to quote you."

"I wasn't thinking that, but now I am," he chuckled.

When they reached their hotel, she texted Jarod before calling.

"Is this a good time to talk?"

He answered, *"Yes."*

London was in his hotel room. It was a perfect time to get into a conversation with Jarod.

"Simone, I could lose my job for this. Even though they never recognized your evidence, your theory wasn't entirely incorrect."

"What do you mean?"

"I think there is a leak in the Bureau. Information was leaked to Mason and his hordes. I believe someone here is working with him."

"What? Do you know who it is?"

"Not yet. They're good at hiding. But listen, I can help you a little. Meet me on the steps of the Smithsonian tomorrow."

"Was I getting too close and they wanted me out? Is that why they fired me?"

"It's hard to say. Look, I can't talk anymore. Meet me at 10 o'clock in the morning. If you can't make it, text me."

As Simone put her phone down, she stared out in space, stunned. After a few minutes, London knocked on her door. When she opened, he noticed her expression and sat next to her.

"Did you call him?"

"Yeah. You won't believe it. He told me he thinks there is a leak at the Bureau. Someone wanted me out. It all makes sense now. We can't trust anyone. If there is a betrayal on the force, it could be really dangerous, more so then I thought."

"That does explain a few things. I know you were already riding a thin line. I can't imagine how much more dangerous it can get."

He stood up and made his way the window, nervously wondering if they had been followed. Should they be watching their backs?

She began to talk out a plan.

"If that person finds out we are here, they will inform Mason and we will be targeted. We should check out early and meet Jarod tomorrow. Maybe he can add to what we already know. He was a good friend and young in the business. I trained with him on some of the worst cases and we went on some raids together. When I left the Bureau, he was the one person who didn't want to see me go."

Neither of them slept well that night. London was in his own room thinking about her plan. She lay under her sheets thinking about what she was fighting for and a tear streamed down her cheek as she cried silently. Finally breaking down, she sobbed herself to sleep.

She woke up in the night with a startled reaction and realized that fear was affecting her body. Her mind raced from one agent to another identifying the behaviors of a traitor. Her thoughts drifted to her father. She wanted to know where he was, was he suffering, what happened to his body? She didn't want to know how they killed him. It would only make her angrier. Up until then, she always avoided the label, but that night she felt like a daughter requiring revenge. She had a power inside her that wanted to be both a talented singer and a super power, bringing her father justice or better, to bring him back to his family. Her mind would not stop thinking of "*what if.*" She was so close that she could almost touch it. If she pushed herself past her limit, she could see sweet freedom in the horizon. Jarod's news gave her hope that her running could soon be over. She wasn't a former FBI agent venting frustrations, she was a daughter who loved her father more than anyone could. Everything she did was for him. She never had to experience sharing him with siblings. It was just her and him. Her encouragement and singing ability came directly from Andrew. Always in the background was his supportive wife, Evelyn. The thoughts made her tired and she slowly closed her eyes.

Penny had been outed, her life and heart were laid out, totally exposed to London. But the woman that night was revealed as Simone Harlow. He wanted to know why she could not tell him her real name. If she trusted him, what was the big secret? He had to admit, there still wasn't much about her life that he knew.

As Simone's thoughts kept her from sleeping, she recalled better days as a carefree young girl living in Italy and living her happiest life.

Chapter 8

Who Was Simone Harlow?

The sun rose on the Italian city of Rome, reflecting a fiery glow across its buildings. From her upper window, she pulled the curtain farther back to appreciate the view. The sky awakened as the sun began casting shadows. In her white cotton gown, she unlatched the windowpane and pushed it open, breathed in deeply, and vowed to never leave. It was what she loved and made her feel her best. Daylight sounds of birds on a light breeze delighted Simone and her fingers combed her hair. After she stretched to awaken, she washing her face in the porcelain basin and folded the soft towel. Walking on the smooth terra cotta floor in her bare feet, she opened her closet to select something for the day. Her style was casual and classy. She was brought up to dress for each occasion when traveling with her family.

She was just a young child when her family moved to Italy, about age five. She missed her friends but was happy to have her parents by her side. A short time passed before she explored the neighboring streets, learning what the Italian lifestyle was all about. She fell in love with the earthy city. Her first memory of Rome was just outside the city. Orchards lined with lemon trees showed off their brightly colored fruit and she inhaled their fragrant blossoms. It reminded her of Limoncello, a favorite of her father's. Italy held an essence of beauty within its culture, something she wished she had known since birth. The women often cooked age-old dishes for their families. Family was everything to them. The aromas of onion, basil, varied tomato sauces, and homemade pastas wafted from opened windows and doorways. With the ability to grow their own vegetables, they felt no need to worry about their next meal. They were mostly hard workers and Simone imagined she was just like them. Only in her dreams, she thought. Cobblestone pathways were bordered by homes built close together. Simone grew to love the perfumed flowers that burst with color alongside their bordered walks.

Her father worked for the United States Consulate and felt honored to relocate to Rome. Andrew Harlow cared as much about the local citizens as he did about his own family. He was qualified and highly skilled in presiding over the affairs of its people. The Consul General followed the Ambassador's lead in the host country and dealt with administrative issues, never viewed as a threat. Although he knew many in his day, Andrew never sought to become a diplomat.

At home, he wanted his daughter to explore everything to discover where her heart belonged. Simone spent a few years as a young child taking ballet lessons only to become more interested in singing. She could hear herself performing in front of the most amazing audiences. It was a natural passion, that no matter where life took her, it would be her first love. It didn't matter where she

105

was, she was singing and humming constantly. Andrew loved to listen in and realized her aptitude. He found the best vocal coach to help her develop and mature, discovering more talent than they realized. She was born with a very special gift. Even though her voice was still maturing, she sounded like she had years of experience.

At thirteen years of age, she took her first lesson and surprised her vocal coach. She demonstrated perfect pitch, tone, and a smooth way of making a song come to life. He watched in awe then challenged her, making songs harder to sing. She learned to hold her notes, breathing from deep within. Some training focused on how to make the song move the listener. She worked on vocal exercises daily and followed her assignments. On top of that, she studied several languages, something her father advised to help her when traveling abroad.

Simone looked like she belonged in Italy, with her clear skin and dark eyes. She was naturally beautiful with a voice to match. A brunette by nature, she always wore her hair long. When she wasn't studying or practicing, Simone enjoyed exploring the neighborhoods and visiting people. Wearing her light sun dress and sandals, her hair pulled back, the sun reached out to kiss her face, leaving light-toned freckles across her cheeks. She enjoyed humming a local tune as she passed by floral shops tempting with her favorite flowers. Nearby neighbors could hear her expressive melodies as she passed by. Everything she saw and heard made her think of music.

Brushing her hair in front of the mirror one evening, she heard a knock.

"Come in."

"I hope I'm not disturbing you," Andrew entered.

"No, I was just relaxing after my bath. I love it here. It just makes me never want to leave." Her eyes gazed out the window as she spoke.

"I'm glad you like it. I was afraid your mother wouldn't like the idea of living here."

"You know she would follow you to the ends of the earth, Dad. She really loves you."

"She is wonderful. I never have to worry about either of you adjusting. I want the best life for both of you."

"I know you care about us. You can see what I love."

"Yes, I can. You were born to sing. If there was nothing else out there, you have a special gift that will carry you through everything you do."

"I've always dreamed of singing in front of famous people, like the Queen of England."

He chuckled, "Don't you think that is a far-fetched dream? The Queen of England is a very big deal."

"It's just my wish. I want to share my voice with everyone. You taught me that."

"I don't want you kept in a gilded cage, Simone. You deserve to spread your wings and fly freely."

She wrapped her arms around him. She was influenced by him to be her very best. At the moment, she realized that no man could ever replace him. He was the one who praised her and expressed faith in her, aiding her to accomplish anything she put her mind to. Their bond was strong and Andrew felt blessed to have his daughter in his life.

For her privacy and because of her father's job, her parents avoided sending her to the public school. Her mother and a tutor adapted to her quick abilities. It surprised them to see that she learned her best without regimented education. She was like a free bird, a girl who wanted to live as a woman, grasping new concepts quickly. She was someone who wanted to spread her wings and get what she wanted out of life.

As a little girl, she absorbed practical wisdom from Andrew. No one compared to her father. Her mother was a good teacher, influencer, and supporter but the relationship between Andrew and Simone was very special. As a teen, she learned about diplomats and ambassadors working with him. He explained the ins and outs of his business, realizing how dangerous it could be. Andrew had seen his share of false visas, passports, as well as stolen ones. She was aware that some people made a living impersonating others; using passports to illegally get in and out of the country for illegitimate operations. The older she became, the more concerned she felt. She was relieved each day when her father came home safe.

When Simone was seventeen, she finished her schooling and her parents gave her a gift for all her hard work. A crystal jewelry case from Ireland made by Waterford. As a child, Simone had been to many countries and collected keepsakes from each place. Ireland was one of her favorites.

She was invited to sing at some of the local pubs and restaurants. The rooms were always filled with regulars and newcomers quickly became fans. Those who worked with her father asked her to sing at their banquets and events. Her voice was soon highlighted before princes, prime ministers, and other European dignitaries. It surprised her to see flowers land at her feet.

It wasn't her dream to play filled concerts with groups of people surrounding her, a record deal, or tour. She had not desired fame. It was in her heart to sing for anyone who would appreciate her gift without the stress of being famous. In time, she still wanted to explore other career options.

Simone was very aware of what her father did day to day. She would listen in on his conversations about criminals falsifying information and who was growing their power and was being watched. Some were known to harm or kill anyone standing in their way. Andrew was unaware, but Simone was intrigued and took in everything she overheard. Thoughts of wanting to keep her family safe, were strengthening. There were times when Andrew expressed his own concern about situations he uncovered. Threats began to arrive from those who were caught and incarcerated.

Simone became fairly well known. The women selling their goods at the edge of town, waved at her as she walked by. She enjoyed her life as it was, but something was missing. Simone had another idea for her life and wanted to talk to her father about her education. For years she had learned how the world was full of violence and sadness. Even though her beautiful voice made people smile, she became obsessed with making a larger contribution to society's well-being. Would her father approve or try to talk her out of it? She had no idea what he would think when she approached him.

Simone first went to the internet for help. Because she loved what her father did, she decided to explore the world of federal investigations. Still, a

US citizen meant a US career. Working for the government would be a challenge and she had no idea how hard it was until researching. An extensive training program and years of study was no deterrent. Since she was already disciplined and educated, she saw no problem with hard work. Secretly, she read up on what she could do to help others. She even researched findings about her father's job as a Consul. It became more than a fleeting thought. She was determined to pursue something she never thought she would take on. She knew she was old enough to go to the States to study. Her parents raised her prim and proper. She was now twenty-three and singing had earned her some money that went into savings. She planned to embark on her journey to fulfill her desire. What she was about to tell her parents would shock them.

She stared out her window reminiscently, recalling how she never wanted to leave her home in Italy. She loved everything about it but was to make a decision that would change all of that. She was ready to tell her father of her plans.

"Dad, can I talk to you and Mom."

"What is it?" Andrew asked.

"I have been singing for quite some time now. I thought about what you said when you wanted me to further my education."

"We thought you would have made a career choice some time ago," Andrew said.

"I had to think about it very carefully, and I have come to a conclusion."

Andrew was excited to hear, but Evelyn was anxious.

"I made prearrangements to enroll you in the finest schools to study music and the arts. Is that what you want?" he asked enthusiastically.

Simone hesitated, "No. I chose a different route." She was pacing and decided to sit down to give them the news.

"I thought you wanted to study music because of your gift," her mother reminded.

"I did, but I have reason to pursue something else."

Simone began to relate her growing concerns for people needing help. She wanted to assist the innocent, clean up the pain that uncaring, hardened criminals perpetrated. They listened without interrupting and Andrew fell in tune with her expressions. He had felt that same way when he chose to be a Consul.

"Well, what is it you want to do?" Evelyn curiously urged.

"I want to be an FBI agent. I have been reading up on what it takes and I know I can do the job."

Their faces were puzzled. They could not picture their daughter as a federal agent.

"FBI? How long have you thought about this?" Andrew asked.

"Over the years I have overheard how dangerous some people can be and how it affects lives. I want to make a difference, just like you do. Dad, what you do at your job is also stressful and dangerous. I learned everything from you and I want to be a savior that helps the public."

"Simone, we can't save everyone or make the world perfect. I know your heart is in the right place, but being an agent is not easy work, I'm sure. It can be life threatening as well."

"I've talked to the academy and applied. They accepted me a few weeks ago and I'm leaving next week for training."

His eyebrows hung low in sadness. "I wish you would have discussed this with us a long time ago. I'm lost for words. It's not like I have another daughter to take your place."

"Dad, I know what I'm getting into. The counselors are very helpful. I know I should have told you sooner, but I didn't want you to say no."

Simone's parents were not the type to argue or shut down her thoughts. Always wanting to encourage growth and exploration, they listened and saw her well-meaning heart. She had a goal in mind to be like her father. He was familiar with the FBI and was concerned for her safety. It was all those years of learning her father's career that gave her the courage to choose.

"You are a grown woman and we can only support your choice." Andrew was trying not to say what he really thought.

"I will always love singing. That will never change. But I need to do this and find my own way to live with purpose. Will you support me on this too, Mother?"

"I will wish you the best of success in your venture, Simone," her mother forced. "I know you've made up your mind but I wish you would think this over more. There is so much you are giving up."

"I'm not giving up singing. I have the chance to do something good for someone who needs me."

Andrew grinned, "Well, look at you. You remind me of myself. I guess I understand why you want this."

After talking it through, they spent the last few days together before she left for the San Diego academy. She made arrangements to live with a friend who used to live in Italy. With the funds she saved, she would pay for her training to show responsibility. Still wanting to take care of her, Andrew put a little extra money in her account.

When the time came to catch her flight, it was bittersweet for Evelyn and Andrew. Simone was their only child and wise enough to know what she wanted. They had to let her go. They could appreciate her motives and let her go without thinking of her as their little girl. The house would be lonely without her sparkle and melodic voice. With a tight hug and a kiss goodbye, Simone left her parents side and boarded the plane to California.

When she arrived, she was prepared to follow directions and learn from her instructors. She went through the formalities in joining the FBI Academy New Agent Trainees, also known as NATs. During training, she spent sixteen weeks with her peers, building a foundation to become a good agent. Simone studied the four major concentrations: Academics, case exercises, firearms training, and operational skills. Her fellow classmates were supportive and became close friends. The counselors and supervisors challenged the students and were uplifting at the same time. With sore and tired muscles, it felt like a boot camp. She mastered pushups, sit ups, and a 1.5 mile run, testing her abilities. A 300 meter sprint was added to the regimented task. At first, she wasn't physically fit enough to ignore the pain after drills. She was often found up to her neck in an ice bath to work through the aches, never complaining. Simone reminded herself that she was a woman of justice, able to save the afflicted and rescue those who fell into loathsome hands. The more she studied about what was required of her job, the more she grew to love it. During warm ups, she would stand in the middle of the field and sing her best, getting it all out. It was a love she would never give up on.

After training was completed, she received her Bachelor's and worked for the Bureau for two years. She was in the best shape of her life and her health evaluations only improved. She felt ready for anything that would come her way, but with her limited field experience, she would do her best. Upon completing her (BFTC), Basic Field Training Course, Simone was assigned to work the Washington, DC office. That made her happy. She remembered her father telling stories about his life growing up in the area.

After working as an agent for another six years, she encountered dangerous cases, sometimes using aggression in the name of justice. Never cruel or emotionally unstable, she was looked upon as one of the best in the DC field. She had reached her goal and felt the satisfaction of making the world one step safer. At thirty, she unexpectedly encountered something not in her plans.

It was the evening her parents had responded to an invitation to an event in Venice. Andrew dropped Evelyn off at the entry and then parked their car. It was almost dark and lights invited her in. She entered a small courtyard sparkling with a centered fountain. Low walls were draped with flowering vines leading from the iron gate. After he locked his car doors, three men approached Andrew, one with a gun drawn.

"Don't make a scene and do as you're told," one man said while gripping his arm tightly.

They forced him into their vehicle and left quickly. Andrew did not return that night. Evelyn waited and then looked everywhere to locate her husband. She called *la polizia municipal*. They had nothing to report. The *ospedale*, hospital in Italian, had not admitted anyone matching his description.

Back in D.C., Simone was completing a file when the call came into the agency. It was deemed urgent.

"Phone call for Miss Harlow, Mr. Boroughs."

"I'll see if she's in the office."

She answered the intercom and picked up the line.

"This is Simone Harlow."

"Si, *Miss Harlow?* This is *il capo della polizia.*"

"Why would the Chief of Police be calling me? Are my parents alright?"

"It is your father. He was at an event for the Consulate and we think he was abducted. We are still trying to locate him but haven't found anything yet."

Simone was quiet, sensing anxiety weaving its way through her body. She had been taught to stay calm and stay strong.

"Where is my mother?" she finally asked.

"She is safe. She was distraught from the circumstances, but we are taking care of her."

"What do you suggest I do?"

"It may be wise for you to come to Italy and console your mother. We don't know why he was kidnapped. We are doing our best to investigate."

She had handled cases like that before but would not be able to use her skills without permission from the Bureau and the Italian Ambassador. Her father taught her that. Simone asked her supervisor permission for an emergency leave.

When she landed, she met her mother at her home. Evelyn wasn't handling the news very well and feared for her husband's life. She was confused why or who would take him.

"Mother, I'm here," she closed the door behind her.

"Simone, I'm so happy to see you." Evelyn's nerves were jangled from all the stress.

"How are you? Have you learned anymore about Dad?"

"Nothing yet. I just keep thinking about an argument your father told me about. It was with Mason."

"I know him. Didn't he used to work at the Consulate?"

"He did. But lately your father has been receiving threatening emails from an unknown source. They never could track them down. I think maybe Mason betrayed him and the Ambassadors."

"How do you know it was him?"

"Of course I don't have any proof it was him but they had that confrontation over a month ago. It didn't end well. When your father exposed him, Mason cleverly hid his activity and avoided contact."

Simone began to ponder the reasons she became an agent, never thinking she would use her skills for her own family. This incident was personal and her father's life was clearly at serious risk. When Evelyn began to cry, Simone felt the urge to step in and take the reins. With her arm around her mother, Simone's mind began a plan of search and attack. Before she got too far, her mother shocked her.

"I believe they killed him."

"Mother, we can't think that way right now. We need to assume he is alive and can be extracted. Let me try to find a way to fix this."

"Simone, be careful. These men mean business and it could get us in a lot of trouble. I need security in my own home and it's frightening here alone at night. I don't feel safe. I'm not sure where to go from here. The waiting is killing me inside."

Simone put her hand on her mother's and closed her eyes. Feeling her mother's pain, it lit a fire inside her to return her father, dead or alive.

Simone paid a visit to the Ambassadors who remembered her as a teenage girl. When she spoke to them about the situation in legal and security terms, they were amazed by her grasp of the situation. They issued recommendations for increasing security to a higher level for Evelyn.

Andrew did nothing wrong to be taken. With all the experience Simone had, it would be a challenge with slim possibilities for rescue. Andrew's daughter would always give it a fighting chance.

She visited the site where he disappeared, took pictures, and asked questions. Someone in the area could have seen or heard something suspicious. Walking the neighborhood, Simone asked everyone if they had seen what took place that night. As she was returning to her car, she suddenly received a tip from a person of interest. She didn't know the informant. He had been listening and watching as she described what she was looking for. He hid in the background but was able to hear something very familiar when she was asking questions to one of his friends. Reluctant to get involved, he changed his mind after thinking it over. He found her in town later that day.

"Excuse me. Can I speak with you? I have something for you."

He was young, a boy who seemed afraid.

"Who are you?" she asked.

"Someone who may be able to help you."

She asked cautiously, "How do I know you are not trying to set me up?"

"I realize you do not know me. But I think I can help you with your goal to find what you want."

"We can talk someplace more private," she advised.

They walked a short way into an alley where no one could hear their conversation. The boy was wearing dirty clothes and his feet showed the wear and tear in his old sandals. As Simone looked upon his face, she wondered how a young boy could live on the streets with no family to care for him. Simone had faith no one was listening as he spoke to her.

The young man assured her that he was reputable and trusted. She started off asking why he decided to come forth. What did he have to do with the disappearance? She withheld information about herself and her relationship with Andrew. She was careful to avoid telling anyone that she was his daughter.

"There is a reason why I am speaking out. I am in fear of my life but want to help. I know the men who took this man you are searching for."

Simone didn't know whether to believe him or not. His voice showed fear, but his stained shirt and homeless appearance led her to pity him. He had the face of a young child.

"How are you involved with the men in question?"

"I used to work for them."

"What did you do?"

"I was just a thief, a pickpocket, you know, stealing from tourists. I started off sneaking petty items and I didn't know they were watching me."

"What do you mean?"

"I was approached by two men who wanted to pay me a lot of money to bring them wallets and purses, anything I could get my hands on that held identification. You know, passports and documents. I was good at not getting caught and they knew that. I have been homeless for years and can't get a decent break or a meal so I turned to crime."

"Have you ever been convicted?"

"No, I was only fifteen at the time and wanted to get out of that life. As soon as I met Mason I considered turning myself in but was too afraid."

"How did you feel when you encountered him?"

"He is controlling and abusive. He is taking advantage of the young boys who steal for him. His operation is so corrupt, letting in anyone who bowed to his power. Illegals are entering into the country and bringing in cartel. This is how he makes his money."

"How did you end up getting out alive?"

"When I told them I no longer wanted to help them, they beat me and threw me out. They told me I was worthless and threatened to kill me. I got away before anything else could happen and went to a shelter. I kept it secret, hoping they would not change their minds and end my life for what I knew. I believe if they find me, I will be their next victim."

Simone did not ask his name.

"Do you know where they are now?"

He knew but refused to take her there. He was afraid and so many thoughts came into his mind wondering if he revealed too much. He was always in danger. He bravely did the right thing and gave her the information she needed. As he scrawled directions, she looked on the troubled young man who needed a better life. She stared at his face with such empathy, wanting to do something to make a difference in the poor soul's life. That was one reason she became an agent to begin with. She could hear the words of her father in her head saying, *We can't save everyone.* She spoke as she was writing down what he knew.

"Do you ever think of giving the police your information? It could help."

He shook his head with fearful eyes. As a former thief, police would easily convict him, if he came forward. He wouldn't take that risk. He was drawn to Simone and hoped someone with better experience and more strength would take them down.

Her heart went out to him. She wanted to protect him, but he assured her he was fine on his own. He knew no other life and only wanted to stay out of sight.

"I hope you find what you are looking for," he said.

"This may be the start you need for a better life," she said hopefully.

"This has been my life since I was young. With my history, I just don't see myself having that kind of dream."

"Thank you for your help."

He left, never seen by her again.

Simone sat inside her car, holding the note in hand. It still felt unreal and made her anxious. Learning what happened to her father gave her stronger reasons to push herself. She casually gauged her surroundings, checking if she was followed or watched. Simone knew she was treading dangerous waters, attempting to enter the operation where the young man mapped it to be. She carefully drove by the building. It looked like a normal place of business. She figured the underground operation should be close by. Locating a rear entrance in the adjoining buildings provided a clue. Where would be the best place to get in undetected?

She would find her way inside and become a trusted part of their organization. To her, it was completely worth the risk. Relying on her training, she quickly left to shop for a perfect disguise. Simone had a knack for creating an unrecognizable persona. New clothes, makeup and wig generated the fictitious woman, Andrea Cole.

Simone was calm but desperate. She knew there was a good chance no authority would approve the case, even though her credentials should prove otherwise. She took a chance and called her supervisor for permission to work in Italy.

"Kenneth, I think I can get help from the government here in Italy. I need to act quickly to find my father."

"I realize this is a personal matter, but you can't go on what some kid told you. It is not enough."

"All I am asking for is permission to proceed. Will you grant clearance or not?"

"Let us look into it a little more before I give you an answer. For now, the answer is no clearance. I suggest you take care of your family business and get back to the States."

"How could you not allow me clearance? Kenneth, you know I am good at what I do. I need to do this!"

"You know the protocol. You cannot do anything before we have enough evidence to go forward. I'm warning you, Simone, don't take the law into your own hands. I think we are done discussing this."

She hung up the phone in disgust and felt anger rise up her neck. Not thinking clearly, she would jump into action in a way her father would disagree with. Simone would dive in head first.

After letting her mother know she was going to be unavailable for a few days, Simone went back. The building looked like a legitimate place of business from the front. There was a receptionist inside the lobby and no hint of criminal activity. Was the boy's map accurate? She questioned if it was the right place.

"Excuse me. Is Mason Banks here?"

"Do you have an appointment?"

"No. I have some business I want to discuss with him."

"Just a moment."

Simone's disguise was created to appeal to someone like Mason. Her makeup and hair color made her attractive, but she carried herself as one to trust.

The receptionist hung up the phone and proceeded to talk to her.

"He will see you now. Take the elevator to the third floor. You'll see a plaque with his name on it."

"Thank you."

As the elevator doors closed she took a breath. She was going to play a part that made her very uncomfortable. She would manage to stay calm and turn on the charm just enough to lure Mason in and still be believable.

"Hello. Will you take a seat?" Mason invited.

"It's nice to meet you."

He looked straight at her, "What can I do for you?"

"I think I have something I can offer you. I would like to be part of your organization."

"How do you know what I do?"

"I got a tip from someone who knows about you. A little smuggling, a little cartel, moving illegals with acquired passports. You have been growing at an attractive rate. Am I wrong?"

He sat upright in his leather chair. She could see his hidden astonishment.

"Your beauty hides what you are about. I would have never suspected a woman like you to be into this kind of work."

"I have skills. What I can do is make you more money with reduced risks. I am good at getting what I want."

"How do I know you're not a spy or working for my competitor?"

"Have you ever heard of a word called, trust?"

"I just met you and you are discussing trust with me?"

"You have nothing to worry about. I know how to stay out of the light. And once I say yes, you can trust it all the way to the bank. Someone in your position can't say no to my offer. I can't get paid by spilling what I know to incriminate you and your group of thieves. You trust the people who work for you. Why not trust someone like me?"

"Feisty. I like that. Do you know how to use a gun?"

"I protect myself."

"What is your name?"

"Andrea Cole. I use my looks and sultry ways to get the job done. Let me be a part of this and you won't be disappointed."

Just then, Mason paged his secretary.

"Susan, send Harry up to my office," he said while still looking at her.

"Right away, Mr. Banks."

When Harry stepped in, he couldn't help but stare at Simone.

"Harry, this is Andrea Cole. She is interested in working with us. She seems to be an expert in the field of getting what she wants."

"We have never had someone so beautiful work with us before. She looks innocent enough to not be suspected." He came closer attempting to touch her face. She surprised them both and swiftly slapped his hand away. He looked back at her, astonished.

Sternly, she explained, "Let's get one thing straight. You put your hands on me and you will have your life threatened, get it?"

"She's cute, Mason."

Mason motioned him out and Harry left the room after winking at Simone.

"I will warn you, Miss Cole. If you betray us or tell anyone about what you see here, you pay with your life. I hope you understand that is how the game goes. I don't want to have to kill someone as gorgeous as you."

"You have nothing to worry about. Shall we say tomorrow? I'll let myself out."

The next day she arrived in the lobby and was sent to another level. It was completely different than Mason's office. The rooms were filled with people who didn't act like paid workers. It was a well-hidden establishment and only a few were allowed to enter and exit through the lobby to avoid undue attention. On her second day, she was shown three back exits, just in case. When no one was looking, she covertly used her small camera. There were times she wandered down the dark hallways, hoping to see her father, but there was enough activity to make it difficult to investigate further. Outside, it appeared that no one knew what she was doing. She was sure Mason would have her followed the first week. It just sounded typical to her.

After her first few hauls her conscience started talking back to her. She kept telling herself that it was the only way to infiltrate and get the evidence she needed. When she retired for the night, she stayed at a hotel a few miles away. At times, she was brought to tears from guilt about getting involved with ruthless people. Mason always seemed pleased after her payoff and thanked her. She nodded and kept the conversation professional while hinting there could be something more. He went for the bait and began asking if she should join him for dinner. She began spending more time with him. He wanted to show her off in public and took her to fine restaurants, clothiers and jewelers. Mason considered himself handsome and having her near him made him feel good. He loved to surprise her with extravagant gifts and beautiful clothes. She played the part of being his love and it disgusted her. What she was doing was working too well. Mason began setting her up with more high profile targets and added a little intrigue to her work day and nights. It turned out that she really was good at getting what she wanted. Mason noticed and began including her in some of his planning. In his office one night, Simone watched him leave the room for a conversation with two henchmen. She quickly scoured his papers and planner. Notes about operations overseas intrigued her the most. One of them targeted Washington DC. What was in Washington that piqued his interest? Could Mason be involved with the US government?

So far, he had not suspected her spying to rescue her father. On the last occasion, Mason was invited to a gala and wanted her to attend alongside. The stress of playing the role was getting to Simone. As she accumulated evidence to catch him, every piece added to her hatred. When she declined the invitation, it infuriated Mason. He demanded she get dressed and go with him, threatening to abuse her physically. Simone was not afraid and smart enough to defend herself. When his control became too much for her, she knew it was time to vacate for good. She reasoned that she had acquired all the information she needed. Why should she continue to fool this man and remain under his control? That night, Andrea Cole disappeared without a trace.

Mason and his men looked everywhere for her and feared the worst. She could turn on him and go the police. That was not the biggest problem for him because he had friends on the force that would laugh at her. But he did not need that kind of doubt cast his way. They could not dig up one small clue.

Simone was over an hour away. Dressed in a white blouse and khakis drinking an espresso, she gathered her latest info into a brief and called Joseph Hastings. A Secret Service agent on the force for twenty-five years, he was one man she could always trust. She told him about her infiltration and evidence, then sent a copy to his email. Joe had always been devoted to his job and cared about Simone. When he heard about what she had done, Joe was sympathetic and cautious. With no family of his own, he had a special fondness for Simone. He agreed to help her and conduct some surveillance on what was going on in the operation.

She picked him up and reached the facility where she estimated her father to be. They noted a vehicle storage yard next to some abandoned buildings. A mechanic shop was operating on the corner. Through a delivery alley, she turned and parked. They both scouted around before hearing something. Over the fence, they saw three men aggressively dragging a man with his hands tied. Simone quickly photographed it. Both were carrying guns and prepared to use them. When Joe shifted to get a closer look, one of the men saw them and fired shots their way. They managed to jump in the car and escape, but not before collecting a bullet hole in the fender. Simone was driving and when they got away, Joe suggested they take another route, in case they were followed.

When she sent over her file with the latest information to the Feds, she thought it better to conceal her relationship with Mason. Instead of receiving praise and justice, the opposite ensued. Simone was reprimanded with consequences. Because of being unauthorized and having a lack of evidence, Simone was fined and let go from the bureau. Both her and Joseph were ostracized. She had to hire Joe's attorney for counsel. Both were told their conduct was unbecoming and broke their oaths to their country and career. Joe, however, would never betray his dear friend in her time of need.

When Mason's place of business was investigated a week later, it was reported as totally legitimate. By appearance, Simone made up the whole thing in blind revenge against whoever took her father. Justice was left incomplete for her and her mother.

Mason and his men did not stop searching for Andrea Cole. They were still in fear of being exposed, expecting it to be just a matter of time. She was on their hit list as a number one target. When a note arrived at the bureau, Joe suggested it was time to quietly relocate to California.

It had been a few months since then that Simone determined to go after Mason again. She hated that she was made out to be inept and unworthy. As an agent, she went beyond and dug deeper than anyone else, with few regrets. She was thankful to Joe for being there but decided it was better not to involve him any further. He had risked himself enough in his career. No one could understand the bravery it would take to go after the gang who may have killed Andrew, except maybe London.

Chapter 9

The Ransom

Jarod waited in the cool shadow of the old brick building. The Smithsonian was well-known for its rich and intriguing history. Jarod knew it well and believed it to be a safe place to meet. No one should suspect an important conversation there. He was jeopardizing his place at the Bureau and risking his reputation for a former agent. She knew Jarod for his quiet and insightful manner. When she worked with him on other cases, he always added additional perceptions that increased their odds. That day was no different. Simone removed her sunglasses and began.

"I'm curious."

"About what? You've been away for a few months. It was like you ran away. Some look at that as a sure sign of guilt. Am I wrong?"

"It's true, I had to hide out temporarily. I needed to gather enough evidence to save myself. Did anyone look for me?"

"I don't know. What about Joe?"

"He has nothing to do with this. He gave me protection like nobody else could."

"Everything points to you, Simone. You have been branded as guilty, a traitor. You can't get your life back by yourself, it's far too complicated. You know that."

Jarod was sincere with his reasoning, but she took it as a subtle warning to let things stay as they were.

"Why are you interested in helping me now?" she asked.

"Because I know some things you do not. After you left, the Bureau was in a mess trying to get things back in order. This is a government agency, everything takes time. You have this idea that if you come in with your experience and your partner, you will be saved. I wish I could help you but we all know better than to get that involved."

"Jarod, you must tell me about the leak. Is it someone we worked with or trusted? If that person knows about my father, then I need to know who it is or what they intend to do. I need information leading to why they took him!"

She was desperately standing her ground and it showed in her eyes. She came so far and nothing was going to change her mind. She had been inside Mason's operation and Jarod felt that she would try again. For a moment, she assumed the man was setting her up. If he was mistrustful, she believed he would not have gone to such lengths to advise her outside of the office. Learning that someone was working inside the FBI, filled her with a new fire and no longer cared about what happened to her. Her eyes penetrated his. She was searching for his motive. "What do you have to do with this so-called leak?"

He knew what she was thinking and attempted to calm her.

His voice lowered, "I am still conducting my own quiet investigation inside the bureau and I don't have all of the answers. I want you to believe I am on your side. We've always made a good team in the past."

She fought back her emotions.

"You really want to help?" She looked up at Jarod with doubt.

"Yes. We both know it is against protocol, but I have my own theory."

"What have you deduced?" she encouraged.

"At first, I thought it was a personal thing with Kenneth. But it goes beyond him. There are two others above him that seem to have a relationship with Mason. He has grown his organization into the same countries they have reached into. You know everyone in the FBI is professional. Professionals like that, work hard not to get caught. I am pretty sure you and your father have been standing in their way."

"I gave everything to the Bureau, everything. I became an agent because of my father and what he stood for. Why would anyone think I was on the wrong side of the fence?"

"You're not. You just can't see your enemies. If you pull this off, I will be amazed. I'm not against you but I just don't see it happening. I'm here helping and risking my badge because I care about you. We learned a lot from each other and that means something."

"I'm not going to back out. Just so you know, I don't scare away that easily."

"Any intel you can dig up will be helpful, but this is not an easy case to figure out. I can see the determination in your eyes. I get it." He had to ask about the man who was with her. "What's with the tall, James Bond guy you're with?"

"That's London. He's good at investigating and I trust him. That's all you need to know, and I'm not interested in romance if that's what you're insinuating."

He tilted his head and peered into her eyes. He read something she did not.

"Don't look at me like that. I know what I'm doing. You know me. I never endanger a case by getting romantically involved." She was standing firm on her words.

"Fair enough."

"Jarod, can I trust you? Can you help me find what I'm looking for?"

"I think I can. If I find out more information, we'll be in touch."

He twisted to walk away and then turned back to add an afterthought.

"I have an idea that you will end up back in Italy."

"Why would I do that?"

"Think about where your father might be, where it all started. Just be careful. We've already talked too long. You have my number. Let me know if you learn anything new. Goodbye, Simone."

He turned quickly and went down the steps, leaving her with disquieting thoughts.

London drove around to pick her up, watching her facial expression for any sign of how it went.

Before she closed the door, London asked, "I was surprised how long that conversation lasted. Did you get the right information?"

"Yeah. He's someone I used to trust."

"Used to trust?" he asked curiously.

"I'm not sure what to believe. He knows something, I can feel it."

"Where do we go from here?"

"How about some dinner? I could use a glass of wine, or two."

She filled him in on the way back, while he often checked his rear-view mirror. The two of them hashed out ways to get into the operation without losing their lives. After the conversation quieted, she thought about talking to her mother again. She needed more about the night her father disappeared.

Upon returning to the hotel to freshen up, she immediately changed into something more casual and comfortable. She knew how to dress up for an occasion, but preferred her favorite sneakers, white T-shirt, and faded jeans. Tying her hair in a soft bun, she removed her makeup to look like an ordinary woman. Inside her head, she couldn't be ordinary. A soft-spoken woman was not going to get the justice she deserved. She could be caring and kind or aggressive and forceful. That was her way.

After they finished their meal, Simone's phone rang. It was her mother.

"Hello, Mother. I was just about to call you."

"I received a message at my door."

"What kind of a message?"

"A notice. It appears to be a ransom note. These men want something that I cannot give them."

"Did you give it to the police?"

"Yes. They tried to find fingerprints and DNA on the envelope but came up empty."

"What did the message say?"

"They want you." Evelyn took a breath, puzzled. "Why would they want you? Do they know your true identity?"

"This is all my fault. I need to fix this."

"Let the police handle this! There is only so much we can do and there are no guarantees your father is alive."

"If I don't do something, I could never live with myself."

She felt anxiety take over her body. She sensed murder from the start but was not prepared to hear it. If they possessed her, how would that benefit them? Maybe revenge for betraying them? She had no time to find answers to her questions.

"Are you there?" her mother prodded.

"Yes, I'm here. I just went to the Bureau. As I suspected, they still want nothing to do with me. But I think I know where Mason is."

"Don't do anything that puts you in more danger. Please, I beg of you."

"I will be safe." It was what she had always said to console her mother and sounded like a line she had memorized for each occasion. "I couldn't get the Italian Ambassadors to let me take the case, given my history, now that I'm no longer with the FBI."

"What does that mean?"

"I'm going to do what I have to do. I will not let them intimidate you or get what they want. That ransom means nothing. They will never have me."

"If you take the law into your own hands, you can go to prison. You were almost convicted before."

"Don't worry, Mom. I want you to stay safe. I may be coming to Italy soon."

"I'm not sure what to do. I really need your father here with me." She was repressing tears.

"I will try to take care of everything. See you soon."

London avoided listening in, respectfully giving her privacy.

"By the look on your face, I can see it wasn't a dinner invitation."

"No. She said they left her a ransom note."

Her voice sounded worried even though she was trying to keep her composure. It was becoming clear how serious their demands were. There was so much to risk and involving London was giving

136

her a feeling of guilt. She wanted to protect him from harm.

"How much money are they demanding?"

"It's not about money. They want me."

"In exchange for what?"

"I don't know. They never wrote anything about an exchange."

"What are we going to do now?"

"We need to go to Italy as soon as possible. London, this is a very dangerous road you are walking with me. If you want to go home, I will be fine on my own."

"I didn't come this far to not see how it turns out." He was trying to make her smile. "No. I want to be here with you."

"But what if something happens? I would never..."

"Don't worry about me. Let me walk with you through the danger. I want to." He was holding her arms to assure her he was staying no matter what happened.

She realized at that moment she was not so tough. She had emotions and fear just like any human would under the circumstances. She should accept that London would always have her back. They were headed to Italy. Life and death were staring at them and no matter the outcome, they were going to get the job done.

Chapter 10

Italy Calls Me Home

Simone had not been home for a few months and felt the excitement flowing through her body as they touched the runway. What would it be like to return to the only place she loved? London had never been off his continent and was sure Simone would teach him some history of the ancient land she called home. As they disembarked, London grabbed her carry-on and followed her through the crowd, letting her get off first. She was quiet as they walked through the airport. Watching the baggage carousel for her other bags, London felt the need to check on her. For a few minutes more, he decided to give her space. It seemed a difficult time for her and her mother. She had told herself that she could not return for fear of putting her mother's life in danger. That thought no longer meant anything to her. She was there and ready to get what she came for. During her stress and anger, she plotted. Revenge crossed her mind. She had mixed feelings about whether her father was still alive that played tricks on her mind. She had to dismiss it all to stay alert in the present with someone she trusted.

London had no idea that his career choice would lead him there. The woman who mesmerized him with her voice was now in trouble and he couldn't give up on her. He could see the parts of her that were frail, hiding behind a veil of strength, never doubting what she could do or how capable she was. He was happy to be the support she needed.

"Are you okay?" he finally asked her.

"Yes. It just seems so surreal. My mind keeps thinking, what if being here accomplishes nothing? I have been dreaming about the day I would get back to being me again. Now it's in my face and I have to say, I'm afraid."

"There is no need to be afraid. You are the most fearless person I have ever known. I have to ask, what would happen if you didn't do this?"

"That's not an option."

"Exactly my point. You have a plan, you have resolve, and there's no turning back. If you did, you would always wonder."

"I know you're right."

Her eyes searched until she found her bags, they walked through the corridor to get their rental car. She could only think about seeing her mother before planning the details of her next move.

"I can see why you love this place so much. It's very romantic," he commented.

"I've always felt that way about Italy," she reflected.

"You make it so easy to beautify this place. How many men wouldn't want a chance like this?"

"The only man I ever let into my world is Joe."

"Tell me a little about him."

"He never married, never had children and no family I know about. Protecting governmental superiors was his only passion. He used to tell me I was the best in the business, better than he was. We got close after this thing blew up and he treated me like his daughter. We were very close to getting the guys who took my father, but we were riding the fringes of death. I just couldn't risk that for Joe. He took me in and has been protecting me ever since. He's a kind man, but never cross him. He treats me like a child sometimes and I find it endearing because he cares about me. It's a part of his gentle side."

"Now that he doesn't have a job, what does he do?"

"He does what any retired man does. He sold his house and most of his possessions with enough money to sustain him for the rest of his life. When this is over, I always want him in my life."

"How did he lose his job working for the Secret Service?"

"We both did what we shouldn't have done. He wanted to get justice for me. When I told him what I was about to do, he stopped me and told me to leave it in the hands of the law. We argued about it until I told him I was going to do it anyway. That next evening, he stepped up and agreed to help. He knew I was just trying to get answers but after we were both found out by our agencies, we were let go. It was all my fault."

"It looks like no one believed either of you."

"Don't forget, Mason is very good at hiding who he is. A successful and controlling crime boss is extremely good at that. He is not stupid."

"What is he like?"

"Handsome, rich, conniving, smart, forceful."

London noticed that her face contracted slightly at her last word.

"Did he ever hurt you?"

"A few times he came close. It was enough to scare me. He would threaten, yell, and grab me by the arms. But it was getting worse and that was when I knew I had to leave."

"I'm sorry for that. Some people know how to yield power over us and it's hard to outthink them. What's our next move?"

"I'll let you know when we stop someplace to unpack."

They managed to stay at an inn near the water that looked like it was built a century ago. The view would be good for Simone.

"This is a great place," London approved.

"I would stay with my mother, but I don't want to put her in harm's way, especially if there is a chance we are followed."

She stood outside, taking in the view from a small balcony. She felt like a child dreaming of the landscapes and started to hum an ancient tune. That was so long ago and too much had happened since. She questioned herself and wondered if she was crossing the line again with the law. No one could understand what it meant to her. It was the most important thing in her life.

"You seem deep in thought," he observed.

"Am I? I just have so many doubts about myself and I don't want to cause more problems with these decisions."

"You can't help who you are. You are a woman who wants justice. You resolved it a long time ago that you wanted to go after Mason. How? I am not sure, but I believe in you."

She stepped sideways and leaned on his arm.

"I know you do."

As they both took in the vista, London brought it up again, "Can you tell me about your name, Penny Rose?"

"What's there to tell? It's just a name."

"I know it's just a name. I'm getting better at reading you and I am full of curiosity."

"It was my grandmother's. She went by Penelope. My grandfather loved her with all his heart and called her Penny Rose because she loved the flower. It was a sweet nickname. They had a beautiful relationship. When she died, he passed a month later. I believe it was from a broken heart. Their love was like no other, so when I went into hiding, I took her name. I still love the sound of it."

"The name reveals who you have loved."

She tried to keep herself from weeping and turned to look at him. He wiped the streams starting her cheeks, she drew closer to him, and gently kissed his lips. Simone let her guard down and broke her own rule."

"Can I tell you something?" he asked.

"Yes."

"I am sorry to tell you this, based on our preset rules, but I love you."

His eyes searched hers for similar feelings.

"I know about your feelings for me."

"Do you think you could...?"

"No, London. I'm actually afraid of love. I've never entertained the desire to settle down and give up all I worked for."

"You don't have to give up anything for me. I see you, just the way you really are."

"Who am I? A woman who is obsessed with getting justice and finding her father? What will I become after this is over?"

"I don't think of you as a woman who questions everything about herself. There is more about you than you know. I loved everything about being in love when my parents were alive. I don't know why I was afraid to find it myself. I don't deal with loss very well. I guess you could say we are the same in many ways."

"True, I don't know where I would be without you here with me. You are part of my life now. When I met you, I never imagined we would be here."

They just stood there holding each other as the scenery surrounded their thoughts. London didn't want it to show but he was afraid to lose her. He couldn't take another loss and the odds were not in his favor. He could only trust that she knew what she was doing. Both were going into the unknown in more ways than one. They were feeling something for each other. Was it support, love, or both? Could it be an attachment for having someone around? It appeared that she avoided analyzing her feelings.

After a pasta dinner, Simone met London in his room. She laid out the plans for her arrival at the operation. He was very adept at studying and memorizing information. She noticed that his mind was quite sharp and could intelligently work through scenarios.

"Let me show you what we're working with. Here is the address. So far, we know about the building and where Mason is expected."

They inspected the map and Simone learned every inch. There was a fire lit beneath her that had some anger behind it. She was prepared to lose her life if she must.

"There are some things I want you to do if I don't make it out alive."

"Why are you talking like this? You're supposed to be my hero, remember? You're not the one whose life ends. You can't think that."

"London, we are professionals and we will have a professional plan. That includes worst-case scenarios too. Now, if I go down, I want you to have a good life. Find a way to be happy again after losing your parents and you can visit my mother if that makes you feel better. Know that we did the best we could. If I die taking them down, it was worth it."

"You won't die. I can't let that happen."

London could see the pain and fear hidden in her words. He had been making silent plans of his own since meeting her. That was the part of him that loved her. He could see that she wanted to be the one applying full force and taking all of the risk. What she couldn't do was left to someone like himself. With everything they had been through, he wanted her to grow the same feeling he was. The thought of her dying for justice saddened his heart.

"There is just one thing," she added.

"What is that?"

"You can't come with me."

"Why?" He was shocked to hear it. "We both came this far together. I worry so much already and now you want to cut me out of it?"

"I care too much about you to risk your life."

"I would risk it for you."

"I know you would. You're just like Joe."

She sat quietly waiting for him to say more.

He sighed, "Okay, if that is the way it must be. I will honor your wishes."

"If things were different, I would want to have you by my side."

"You know I would be there in any situation. You can always count on that."

There was nothing left to say. London wanted more quality time with her before she jumped into the fire. He had drawn close to her but an ache in his heart told him that she could not give herself to him, or anyone. She had so many things to do in her life before settling down. What if neither of them could fulfill a love because of their career and trauma history?

He watched her get up to brew a cup of tea in the kitchenette and whispered to himself, 'Just stay alive Penny and then change your mind about us.'

The next day she took London to meet her mother. She avoided disclosing their plans, but Evelyn knew her determination and asked to speak to London privately.

"I'm sure she informed you on how she wants to find her father," Evelyn warned.

"Yes. She has a passion that I wish I had. My fear is that she will fail again, and I don't want that for her."

"She was never like this as a child. She was set on being a singer and loved nothing else than to make people smile. She and Andrew were very close. When she learned about what his job entailed, something was lit inside her. She wanted to be like him in so many ways. When he was kidnapped, it just fed that fire even more. I fear for her life just like you do." Evelyn studied his eyes, "I can see you have a special love for her too."

"Does it show? She doubts herself so much that she may never want love from me or anyone. We have connected and neither of us expected it to go that far."

"Give her some time. She might come around. From the day she was born, she had to do things her way."

"Let's hope that it works in her favor." He tried to sound assuring, although he was less than positive.

That evening, London pondered the first day he met the singer who took his breath away. In his mind, he could hear her name announced while he sat at the bar. Images of her were still vivid in his mind, her smile, her laugh, her beauty all told the story of a woman unwilling to faulter. When he learned of the ransom, he wondered what they wanted and what would be exchanged. It had to be serious. Because he would rather picture her on stage, he fell asleep to his dreamy image of Penny Rose.

Morning came and London rapped on Penny's door to have a coffee with her. When she did not answer, he noticed her text.

"Went for a walk. Be back soon."

She was strolling the cobblestone alleys where she used to roam and relived her past, longing to return to simpler times. Could she ever go back to singing? She had a lot to think about. Walking under the old trees, she stopped to enjoy the newly blossomed flowers. Their soft fragrances always captivated her imagination. At the water's edge, she closed her eyes to picture the young schoolgirl learning all of the innocent things in life. The sun peeked between lemon trees and the smell of warm grapes on the vine moved her to capture their essence with her camera.

Those were moments lost when she became an agent. It was drilled into her to develop a strong and hard edge. Recently, the tough exterior was evaporating. Her frail and delicate side was being exposed. Unexpectedly, thoughts of London appeared and led to questions. What was she feeling for him? Was he more than a friend, someone she could give her heart to? More than once she caught herself smiling when he walked in. Before going to bed, she had to shake off the irresistible mystery. While she believed that he was a good man, he had an obvious weakness. London

147

still could not completely care for himself. He needed to deal with his own issues before thinking about taking a wife. He was still dealing with his loss. When he talked about the closure he needed, it was something she understood. No matter how strongly they felt about each other, there was always a gap that needed to be closed. She tried looking at the bigger picture by taking everything into consideration. What would shape her life and the life of London? If she came out of it alive, she knew that her life could be fulfilling. As far as a relationship with London, she would always care for the man who took the journey, willing to lay down his life for her. She was grateful for his devotion, but was it enough?

Chapter 11

Good Conquers Evil

London was going over his plan throughout the night. He didn't get much sleep, wondering how to convince Penny not to meet with Mason. She planned a surprise attack alone, forcing him to make auxiliary plans she couldn't learn about. To protect her, he made up his mind and reached her room, hoping it wasn't too late.

"Penny, open the door. It's London."

"What is it?"

"I want to talk."

She let him in and the door automatically closed behind.

"I know what you want to say."

"If you know this is too dangerous, why are you going about it this way? You are not even sure if your father is still alive."

"I have to believe he is. You don't know how long I have needed to take these men down. Before I met you, there was a determination in me that hasn't

149

gone away. Just because you are here now and want to stop me, doesn't give you the right to tell me how to do it!"

"I'm not telling you what to do! I'm asking you to be sensible! You're not even following your training. You're not leading with your head."

She crossed her arms and walked to the other side of the room. He followed and stood in front of her.

Softly he urged, "Listen to me; you may not come out of this alive. They may take everything from you and then what? Be left with the exact same results as before? You may have been the best in the force but that doesn't mean you are skilled enough to take down harden criminals like Mason without assistance."

London was containing his frustration.

"I don't care. If there is something I can do to get justice, I will fight anyone to get it, even you."

"Remember that I'm not against you. I wish I could take them on for you and you know I would do it!"

"I wouldn't let you. I can't let you get into my head, London."

"Are you listening to yourself? You could go the police with this and they would..."

"Would what? Wait for them to make this into a slow-moving case and then where will I be, back to square one? I have waited long enough and I am finally going to do this my way."

"Even if it means spending your life in jail? You are going beyond what any human can do!"

"I loved being an FBI agent more than singing. I never thought I would feel that way but so many times I helped catch some of the worst people on the planet. I can't back out now."

"Do you think it would be cowardly to adjust your tactic? No matter how long it takes, local law enforcement handles it better than we can. Why can't you see that?"

"I've lost faith in the system. They may give up everything to make the world a better place but it doesn't help me. For so long no one heard my cries for help."

He stepped back until she could see his eyes. He lowered his voice.

"The day I saw you, I heard. I listened intently to every word."

He saw her expression soften and he placed his finger on her lips.

"There was something about your voice and the way you stood your ground that made me want to listen to everything you had to say and I have been there for you ever since."

She turned her face away, "I noticed. You knew this was risky and you knew I am going to listen to my heart."

He put his hands on her arms and had her face him. "Look at me. When we met, I observed a beautiful woman who pushed aside anyone who got in her way. That woman was talented and knew how to get what she wanted, most of the time. I know this is who you are. You have your whole life ahead of you to waste it on a theory that does not always work."

"I have to take that chance. If I succeed, then my job will be done. I can go on with life knowing I tried. I will die of a broken heart just like my grandfather if I never act on what I know is right."

"What's the real reason why you don't tell me your name?"

"What does that have to do with anything?"

"Maybe you are hiding something I don't know about, Simone."

He could hear her breath as she lifted her face in surprise.

"What did you call me?"

"Simone. If you trusted me and you brought me this far to ambush that circus of criminals, you would have been straight with me. What are you trying to forget?"

"I have nothing to hide from you. How did you find out?"

"You left your passport on the bed."

"You went through my things?!"

"Just your passport. I want to know you."

"Why? Why did you do that?"

"You can't see it? I would go to the ends of the earth for you and you have no idea how this is killing me that you might toss me aside for your own satisfaction."

"You seem to be forgetting this is my fight!"

'Then why did you bring me along? You talk about dying and not making it out alive and you expect me to feel no anxiety. I am afraid to lose you."

"When I think about being Simone, I feel a pain of never getting those days back in my life. Maybe Simone doesn't want to exist."

"No, she's still here where she grew up. You are filled with wonderful memories with every emotion. I know a lot has changed for you but you don't have to throw any of it away. I don't want you to lose your happiest days."

"I've been shot at, grappled with the strongest felons in the most horrifying places. My life has been on the line so many times and I learned not to let it shatter me. This may not be your way, but it surely is mine."

London was unsure if he was angry or disappointed. The woman he cared about was hurting and wrong. He turned to the door with one last thought.

"I don't know exactly what will happen. But if you never come back to me, I will always remember the woman who changed my life and made me a better man. I will never forget what you have done for me, Simone Harlow."

She stared, not following. He searched her face for a brief moment and walked out. She couldn't think of anything to say. She stepped out onto the balcony, wondering if he was right or was just thinking with a romantic heart.

London remembered always thinking of her as a super woman. Now she was the one needing someone to step in and heroically rescue her from the flames of death.

Early the next day, Simone parked a few blocks from Mason's operation. Between darkened structures, she found a back door. It was not tightly closed. Unseen, she slipped in to find a concrete staircase. She recalled something about the third floor. It was busy. Simone immediately stepped into character and acted like she belonged. Walking past several employees, no one recognized anything out of the ordinary. She was in casual street clothes, and her hair tied in a ponytail. From a doorway, Harry suspected something as he noticed a new woman asking the receptionist for Mason. He followed her quietly until she disappeared into the office.

When she stepped inside, he was sitting behind a large desk looking down, unaware of her presence until she slammed the door behind her. For a moment, she fought back her disgust.

Mason lifted his head, "Excuse me, do you have an appointment?"

"No. I don't think I need one."

She let down her hair.

"Well, Andrea, or is it, Simone Harlow? You have returned. I can see my partner did his part drawing you out of hiding. I'm sure you liked playing the part of a sultry woman enticing me."

"You sent the ransom note."

"Indeed I did."

"How did you know who I was?"

"I'm not stupid. Oh, it took a while, but I figured it out, Andrew's daughter. My men have been looking for you. There was no Andrea Cole to fit your

154

description. I must say, you are very good at hiding and using an alias. You could have worked for me and done quite well for yourself. It's too bad your looks were so deceiving."

"Who am I, Mason? A young woman with a disguise taking down your organization?"

"Is that what you wanted to do? You were a part of it too, you know."

"You set me up. You turned the people I trusted against me."

Smiling, he got up from his chair and touched her face.

She turned her face and forced his hand away.

"You betrayed me. You got what you deserved and now you are here to get revenge."

"Where is my father?"

"Why should I give you any information about the man who turned against me? You were not the only one who was hated by someone you trusted. Your father could have been a rich man and we could have done it all together. But he decided to turn against me and turn me in to Interpol. I just couldn't have that happen."

Just then, Harry walked into the office with a gun tucked in his belt.

"I saw her come in and followed her," Harry said.

With her strongest voice, she asked, "Is my father alive?!"

"Take Miss Simone out of my office. Don't put up a fight. Harry's not a very nice man."

Mason walked behind them through a dirty hallway to an elevator that opened in a warehouse with parked cars and vans. It was an obvious business front to hide where the real money was coming from. They stopped in view of a dusty office with bars on the window. Simone knew it was the wrong time to resist. She stood her ground and waited to see what they planned.

Harry pulled Simone closer to him by jerking her arm. She pulled her arm back and turned to sneer at him.

"You smell very bad. It's like you crawled out of the sewer."

"You better watch your mouth," he said as his hand reached for her face."

Mason broke his silence by clearing his throat.

"Maybe you would like to see why you came here."

A guard brought out a thin blindfolded man with tied hands. His clothes were dirty and torn.

"Do you recognize him?" asked Mason.

"No."

"Take off the blindfold."

When the guard removed it, the man tried to focus his eyes to see where he was. He was weak and frail and dropped to his knees. At twenty feet apart, he was difficult to recognize in the dimly lit structure. After looking a little deeper, she could see his features. It was Andrew.

"Father!" she cried out, pulling against the man holding her back.

"Simone!" he cried out in a weak voice.

Andrew was unable to call out to his daughter with any force. By contrast, Mason's voice came out strong and smooth.

"You both caused a lot of problems. With what you know, you could go to the authorities again and try to turn us in. But we can't let that happen. Isn't it amazing how the tables can turn on someone you once trusted?" mused Mason.

Just then, the sound of a car door opening turned their heads. A well-dressed man stepped out of an SUV, staring right at Simone. Her heart dropped. She knew immediately who it was.

"Jarod? You're part of this?"

"The woman who claimed to be the best in the business. You're so stupid. You will trust anyone. But it wasn't just me who turned. We managed to get others in the FBI to join us and you kept getting in the way."

"You? You're the leak? You who got me fired! How could you do something so low?"

"Mason makes good offers and I can't refuse him. If that means taking down our best agent who also happens to be the daughter of the enemy, well that's beauty."

Mason took control, "Simone, I want what you took from me. Return the photographs and microchip now."

"Do what you have to. I will never cower to you."

Andrew insisted, "Simone, give them what they want."

"No, Father. They can no longer intimidate us. We will not give them their way."

The sound of Mason's leather shoes against the dirty concrete announced his determination. When he came near, he locked eyes with Simone. Suddenly, he slapped her face with the back of his hand. It could be heard in the warehouse. She was determined and held her head up strongly. He motioned to bring Andrew near, allowing him to stand next to Simone. Holding tightly, she expected the worst. She felt like death was coming for them and there was no way to escape. It was not any better than the last time she did it alone. Was that how it would always turn out when no one could be trusted? Her father took hold of her arm to keep himself from falling to the ground. She held him, supporting his weight. How could she get what she came for with a limp father in her arms?

Mason nodded again and his men stood them in front of a wall. As they clutched each other, Simone could feel her father's tension. Was it the last time they would hold each other? All was silent except for Mason's cynical voice.

"Kill them," he commanded.

Harry and the guard pulled weapons out of their holster and removed the safety.

Along one side of the warehouse was heard a squeaking door and on the street side the bay doors rolled up. Through the sunlight, eighteen armed officers marched into the warehouse. Simone was shocked to see London among them, front and center.

"Drop your weapons now!" an officer shouted through a bullhorn.

London added, "I would do as they say. You see, they have the place surrounded and your henchmen have been captured."

She was surprised to see London leading the pack of soldiers who were part of a SWAT team. Simone and her father never moved from their spot to stay safe.

The men dropped their guns. While the officers were cuffing and searching their captives, lying flat on the ground, Jarod was still standing away from the commotion. Watching London lead a foil against his plot irritated him enough to speak out.

"You should have minded your own business. It was never about you. You had nothing to do with it," Jarod warned. He then slid a gun out from under his jacket and pulled the trigger. Simone watched in horror as London fell to the ground.

"London!" she gasped as she tried to move toward him. Andrew held her back, protecting his daughter. She was trying to wriggle her way loose to get to him.

Andrew could not retain her long because of her strength. Simone's training automatically kicked in. She rolled and grabbed the dropped weapon nearest her and aimed.

"Don't make me use this. You ruined my life and now you will pay!"

"Simone, put down the gun," one officer shouted.

"No! They are the bullies who tortured my father."

Just then, Jarod swung his piece at Simone.

Before she could pull the trigger, a shot was heard and a second later Jarod joined London face down.

Mason was grabbed and taken into custody. Large black vans pulled in and were loaded with those apprehended, one of the larger takedown's in Italian history. After a few minutes, Jarod's body was lifted into an ambulance. Simone ran to London's side.

"You gave up everything for me," she said while holding his limp hand where her tears landed.

Suddenly, his chest started rising. London opened his eyes and began to move.

"You're alive?"

She lifted his head. The wind had been knocked out of him and he was a little dizzy.

"You're alive! How is that possible?" she asked in disbelief.

London got on to his knees, "I came prepared. I asked the police to let me in and they protected me."

He opened his shirt to reveal a bulletproof vest with a silver slug. She couldn't help but reach for him and wrap her arms around his back. Tears stained his shoulder.

"I thought I lost you. I couldn't bear the pain of losing my friend. You risked so much and you saved us."

"I had been planning to send the police at the right time. We worked together on it. I couldn't let you do this alone. It wasn't right."

"Somehow, I could feel your concern was here with me. I thought you might be the one to save me."

"I wanted to return the favor."

"Who is this brave young man, Simone?" Andrew asked.

"Father, this is London Taylor. He is now my saving grace and a light in my life. He is also my good friend."

"Thank you for what you did. I am forever in your debt for rescuing my daughter."

"I couldn't have done it without Simone."

The paramedics examined Andrew and put an IV drip in his arm to nourish him. He had some bruises and cuts that needed attention and was half starved. Simone knew that her father had been through a lot for the few months he was under Mason's control and would need physical and psychological help. Just looking at him magnified the gravity of what thugs did to people who wanted justice like she did.

London was still having pain in his chest from the blow. Simone helped him to his feet and walked next to him, concerned.

He turned to her, "I'm sorry for what I said to you in the hotel. I was terrified at the time and wanted you safe. That was my promise when you told me about your plan."

London words were heartfelt.

"I knew what your intentions were. Words can never say how grateful I am for your commitment to me. It saved my father from death. I was shocked to find him alive."

"In all my years as a detective, I never thought I would take on a case like this. I was happy to be part of your journey.

He leaned in and kissed her while she adjusted her blanket.

"Those officers are going to interrogate me for this."

"I know. You are ready to plead your case. You have everything you need."

"It's hard to believe after everything we've been through, it's not completely over yet."

"Relief is coming. You will be free soon."

"Miss Harlow. Your father is slowly improving. We are going to take him to the hospital now, for an evaluation and get him on the road to recovery."

"Can I go with him?"

"You may go with him. But be aware, the authorities will be asking you some questions about what you know. It's really a miracle that you made it out alive, thanks to your friend here."

After Simone and London left from the hospital, two policemen met them at the station to file reports and answer the detectives questions.

"It's different being on this side of the table," London remarked.

They gathered details about Simone's involvement with Mason and the FBI, trying to look at it legitimately, without judgement until a trial. After questioning Simone, they warned her she had no legal authority to be there. She realized she would have to plead her case in court and bring out what she knew about their black organization. She would have to mentally prepare herself for a trial. Could she redeem herself and get her life back? At that time, she wasn't sure. She was released and later received her summons to appear. Down that road, justice was in the distance, redemption was calling her name, and relief was not easy. Simone would spend some of her days in an Italian courthouse, not expecting them to go easy, since their laws were different than the United States. She could be looking at jail time, a fine, or both. Whatever the outcome, she was happy her father could go home where he belonged, with his wife. London was uncharted and she was unsure if he would he stay for her trial. His devotion might have a limit.

Chapter 12

A Choice Comes With a Price

Simone had received her trial documents through her legal advisors and gathered all she needed, including her files for a thorough investigation. It took weeks to carefully identify everything to present her case logically. There were stolen ID cards, driver's licenses, visas, and passports along with information from their computers. Her team documented DNA samples and pictures from the crime scene where they found Andrew and Simone. A few suspects turned up missing and were declared murdered by the mob. Simone learned of the four who worked for the FBI that were arrested and extradited to be tried in the US. It made her sad to think that those she once worked with, betrayed their oath and chose loyalty money over their jobs. Jarod slyly influenced them to become criminals.

London was not found to be a person of interest but gave them what he knew and he was cleared of involvement. Simone was disturbed that it made the papers and the public learned about her and what she had been through. Locals were supportive because they knew of her when she was a singer.

Others were shocked to see she had a secret life. She was willing to go through the process, hoping that those loyal to her would welcome her back. The newspaper showed a picture of Andrew, disheveled and dirty upon being rescued. Many of the members of the Consul were stunned to learn of the abuse because he was known as a kind man. Simone was not comfortable that the photographs were made public but was happy to have a living father and consoled mother. That was worth everything.

London was in his hotel room when his cell phone rang.

"Hey, Sully. It's good to hear from you. What time is it there?"

"Not even lunch time. Hey, you texted me that you are in Italy and I just had to see how you're doing."

"I'm better. I was going to come home but I want to stay here with Simone and support her."

"I saw the news. You should be proud of yourself. You helped take down one of the largest criminals out there. Did you ever think it would be possible?"

"No. The woman I met back home at the bar gave me what I was searching for all along. She helped me find out who I really am."

"I could see that person and always have. What's going on with your business?"

"I have been forwarding my client's emails and phone calls. Berkely is taking my prospects until I return."

"I'm glad it's over and you're safe. Let me know when you return."

"I'd like that. I can fill you in on the details."

London caught a ride to the Harlow home. He was happy to learn of their health, reminding him how blessed Simone was to have them.

"London, please come in."

"Thank you, Evelyn. How is Andrew?"

"He's resting but the doctor said he'll be fine."

He began to ask a question, "Is Simone here?"

"She is. She's in the garden. Just go out these doors and you'll see there."

As he walked out, he could caught her resting on a chaise lounge chair. Her hair was down and was barefoot. She looked comfortable next to a glass of wine on a small table.

"Hey," he announced timidly.

"Hi. I thought you were going to head home."

"No. I changed my mind. I think it's best if I stay here with you. You know, for moral support."

"Moral support. Don't you think it goes deeper than that?"

"Maybe. The truth is, I want to be here."

"I just keep thinking about the trial. My name is still in the gutter and I want to be heard."

"Well, you have a lot to say. I can understand that but most of that's behind us now. You are not used to going forward, are you? Life is supposed to only get better from here."

She brightened up, "My father is getting stronger and gaining strength back. He still hasn't told me what he went through when he was missing. But I think he feared for his life every minute he was there. I can't wait to see him back on his feet again."

I'm sure my parents won't mind if you stay at home with us during the trial."

"Oh, I shouldn't impose."

"You're not. To me you are the real hero to this story."

London decided not to reply and instead watched her hair blow lightly in the wind. It was one of those rare moments he remembered her calm and at peace.

She smiled and then looked away for a moment.

He spoke up, "You know, you got me drinking wine now."

"Really? What made you change?"

"Nothing in particular, just thought I'd try it."

"You kept your options open. Good for you."

"I did more than that. I decided to be a part of your world. It's beautiful because I am there with you."

"You make it look like a perfect match," she sneered.

"The dynamic duo, remember?"

"We are a good fit."

"Hey, if you are acquitted, will you go back to the FBI?"

"I couldn't say. So much has changed since this began. Like you, I am keeping my options open."

All he could come up with was, "That's a good place to start."

"I will get back to you about staying here, then we can discuss dinner. How does that sound?"

"Wonderful, talk soon."

Why were things so strange between them? They both kept wondering how many things had changed after their challenge was reached and the air cleared. Did romantic feelings always die after the heat of the battle cooled?

When London arrived at his hotel, Simone messaged him that her parents approved his stay with her family. Before checking out of the hotel, he decided to make a phone call to Kenneth Boroughs at headquarters.

"Hello, I'd like to speak to Mr. Boroughs."

"One moment, please."

"Kenneth Boroughs."

"Hello, Mr. Boroughs. This is London Taylor. We met when Simone Harlow tried to talk to you before we were rudely thrown out."

"What do you want, Mr. Taylor."

"I'm sure you read the papers and saw the news."

"Yes. You're the one who became the hero. Simone did nothing. She may still get what she deserves."

"You don't know enough about her to say that. What she did was not any different than when she was with the force. She was devoted to her job as an FBI agent. She loved it. She is talented and the risk she took saved her father's life. You know some of your own agents were part of the scheme? That is embarrassing, isn't it? And Simone remained innocent."

"Are you trying to get her job back?"

"No. I'm saying this because she was on the right path the whole time. Her father shaped her into the woman she is and she wanted to repay him for that. You made her feel like her life with the FBI was a sham and she was involved with crooks. Well, I'm here to remind you, you were wrong. Now, she's going to trial and after she wins, I hope she shoves it in your face. She will get her life back. As for you, you will have that on your conscience all your life. I hope you realize where your actions led you and your team, which is nowhere."

London hung up the phone without waiting for a retort. He didn't want to hear Kenneth have the last word. It was on his mind and he felt good getting it out. Kenneth was too proud to admit that she was innocent. London just wanted it put it in front of him to realize he can't mess with someone's life that way.

After weeks of questions and examining photographs, she was prepared by the best attorneys in the business. Her father made sure of that. The time came for Simone to attend her first trial date at the Italian court.

When defendants were brought in to present their pleas, they all heard Mason's plea of not guilty. It stunned Simone to think he really believed he was not part of the operation. She had hard evidence to prove he was the one who shared his plan with her and had photographs that should clear herself. The investigators took all that into consideration without prejudging. When the arraignment was completed, it was time to go to trial.

That morning, the courthouse filled up with observers behind Simone and her attorneys. She was dressed in a fitted black dress with a bolero jacket of the same color. Her brunette hair was down, draped over her shoulder, softly curling at the ends. She was ready to explain what she was doing at the warehouse where the ambush took place.

"All rise. The honorable Judge Bernardi is presiding," the bailiff announced.

Simone knew how to present herself. When the judge spoke, London was sitting in the back listening to every word. The proceedings commenced,

"I'd like to call to the witness stand Miss Simone Harlow," the attorney announced.

"Have a seat, Miss Harlow."

She wasn't nervous. It wasn't like the last time when she was blindly accused of being a traitor. London could picture the lights dimming with her breaking out in song. It was time to tell her whole story.

"Miss Harlow, can you tell us what your involvement was with Mason and his business?"

"I knew little about him. He was a friend of my father's."

"What made you want to go to the warehouse that day?"

"I wanted to retrieve my father, find out where he was or if he was still alive."

"You know making that move could have ended up with you losing your life."

"I know. I was familiar with Mason and his operation. I learned where he moved from a tip."

"Where was this tip from?"

"It was from a young man. I didn't know his name. He was someone who worked for petty cash, stealing passports and identifications."

"Where is this young man?"

"I don't know."

"Did you return to that place to reconnect with Mason?"

"No. Even when I first had an encounter with Mason, I hated him."

"Well, hate's a strong word. Were you out for revenge?"

"At first I thought I was, but no. I just wanted my father back home."

"So, you had no involvement with Mason or his men when you entered?"

"No."

"Your witness."

A tall young man in a shiny suit stood up.

"Miss Harlow, is it true that you used to be Mason's lover?"

"I pretended to be his love interest. I wouldn't say we were lovers."

"You were caught working for his mob in the past and you were found to have been involved. Why is this time so different?"

"I wanted nothing to do with Mason's business. I just wanted to find my father."

"So, you broke the law? You admit you were part of it?"

"No!"

"Objection your Honor."

"Overruled."

"Miss Harlow, you put others in harm's way. Like Mr. London Taylor. What was the reason for that?"

"He is a detective in the States. We met there and he agreed to help me."

"You are fortunate he wasn't an accomplice to your crimes."

"There was no crime. I only wanted to get what belongs to me!"

"And your friend was shot. He could have been killed."

"He's alive. He risked his own life for me, on his own terms!"

"That's what you want to believe? You have a record, Miss Harlow. You were kicked off the force at the FBI for a reason."

"I was let go for the wrong reasons. I wasn't convicted of any crime."

"Not yet," the prosecutor assured.

"No further questions, your Honor."

"You may step down, Miss."

Andrew agreed to take the stand and go into detail about what those few months were like under Mason's control.

"I would like to call Andrew Harlow to the stand."

Simone had asked her father to wait to testify but he felt he was strong enough to get justice for himself. This one was going to be his.

"Mr. Harlow, How long have you worked for the Consulate?"

"Over twenty-five years."

"Did you start out working in the States?"

"I applied to work as a Consular Fellow to become a Foreign Service Specialist. To meet all the requirements, I was able to speak four different languages, that includes Italian."

"Did Mason Banks work alongside you?"

"Yes. We became good friends."

"What was the troubles you two were having before you were kidnapped?"

"He wanted to make a deal with me to use my job to let illegal aliens into the country and expand to other areas. Since I dealt with passports and visas, he thought I would be a perfect candidate."

"What did you do then?"

"I warned him and said I would not do anything stupid. I could not betray what I have worked hard for, just for money. I later found out he was just befriending me because I was a Consul."

"How did you respond?"

"I told him I would take what I knew to the authorities. He threatened me and told me he would kill my wife and ruin my life. After I accumulated my information, they forced me into their vehicle and imprisoned me."

"What do you go through while you were in their custody?"

Andrew had to take a breath and gather his thoughts. What he went through was horrific and terrifying. He was still dealing with the trauma and fear during those frightening months.

"Take your time, Andrew."

"They kept me in a dark room, feeding me stale bread and water. The place was dank and lonely. Occasionally they would let me out to interrogate me and convince me to join their brood. When I asked them why they were keeping me alive, they said we are using you to draw out what we really want."

"What was that?"

"Simone. They wanted my daughter."

"How did that make you feel?"

"They beat me so much, mistreated me, and then I no longer felt the blows. I just kept thinking about my daughter and how much I wanted her safe. Today, I am grateful she saved me from the horrid conditions I was in and how I was treated. They planned on killing us together."

"Thank you, Andrew. I know this is difficult."

The judge asked the defense if he had any questions. He replied no. Andrew was able to step down with a face showing his pride in Simone.

Other witnesses were questioned and cross-examined. Each one mentioned how Mason controlled most of the operations at the warehouse and their lives were often threatened if they betrayed them. A few didn't know anything illegal was going on. Simone's attorney wanted to question her one more time and recalled her to the stand.

"I recalled you because I wanted to ask a few more questions."

"Alright."

"The US case you were involved in was closed and no fault was found with you. Also, you were fired because of the very same case. Is this true?"

"That's right."

"Did you know about the leak in the force?"

"No. Not until Jarod told me about it."

"When was that?"

"When I was in the States, just before coming here. I never imagined he was part of it until he showed up at the warehouse."

"Do you feel like it was wrong to fire you from the FBI?"

"I think I could have been disciplined for my actions. But fired, no. I think I was wrongly let go."

"You had no firearms or weapons of any kind when you went to see Mason. Did you have any intentions of killing him?"

"No. I made the sacrifice for my father. Mason requested a ransom. That was all. I was willing to give myself up for my father."

"We just received this letter from the Federal office in Washington DC. They wanted to let you and everyone else know that there was a thorough investigation and you were wrongly let go. They are presenting this letter of apology to you." He handed the letter to her.

"Thank you. But I guess it doesn't matter what they say about me or my actions, I don't have a future working for them, even if they decided to take me back."

"Do you want to see Mason behind bars?"

"Yes. When I saw my father and the way he looked, I knew they abused him. I have never seen him look so emaciated. The abuse changed him. He doesn't talk about it with us.

"Thank you, Simone. You may step down."

When she stood up, she could see London watching, like when she was on stage. He smiled knowingly.

The attorneys made their final statements. Each word was expressed too slowly for Simone.

"We will recess and wait for the jury to give us their answer. Court is adjourned."

She shook the hands of her attorneys and walked between observers to find London.

"You are on your way to being free."

"I think you're being presumptuous. I don't think I'm going to jail but I may be fined. I shouldn't guess what will happen."

"It will be alright."

The preliminary hearing showed there was plenty of evidence to convict Mason on many counts. He had his day in court along with his henchmen. They carefully looked at everyone's testimony. It would be one more relief for her and for London. Her dream to have this be over was finally coming true.

After waiting a few hours, the court was back in session. The jury had made their decision.

"Ladies and gentlemen, we are still in court. Be seated."

The judge turned to the jury and asked the burning question,

"Have you reached a verdict?"

"Yes, we have."

"What is your conclusion?"

"We find that Miss Simone Harlow is not guilty of committing a crime."

"That is the final word of the jury. Miss Harlow, you are free to go."

Free to go. To her, those words overwhelmed her to tears. All she wanted to do was go to London and be wrapped safely in his arms. She no longer wanted to be inside the building.

"Let me take you home," London said.

"I'm free."

"You came to do what you planned and I'm proud of you."

As she left the courtroom, the press were outside the doors with cameras, wanting a statement. With her sunglasses on, she didn't need to defend herself anymore. There was no need to explain herself or lay out her evidence for the presentation. That part of her life was completed. She knew and that was enough for her.

All the way home, it was quiet in the car. London wanted to say something but surmised that she was not speaking for a reason. She was collecting her thoughts and showed signs of exhaustion. They pulled into the driveway of her parent's home. He wanted to open the door for her but she was quick and hurried to the house. When she approached the door, they were there to meet her.

"Do you have any news for us?" Andrew asked.

"Not guilty. The decision was not guilty. Not even a fine. I never thought this day would come."

Her parents couldn't stop embracing her. London could picture their affections when she was a child.

Andrew drew back a step and addressed his daughter, still wrapped in her mother's arms.

"I appreciate all you did for me. But I hope this never happens again. I love you too much to think of losing you."

"I have learned so much from this experience. I should have never acted in desperation but it brought you here to me. London has been trying to talk me into relying others. Thank you, London for being there for me."

"My greatest pleasure."

They went inside for a tea and related all of the twists and turns they went through. Andrew was putting on weight, continuing his therapy sessions, soon to be released by his doctors to go back to work. Evelyn would miss him being around the house during the day. It was a forgone conclusion that Mason was headed to prison and would no longer bother Simone or her family.

The next morning, Simone and London had breakfast in the courtyard together. Afterwards, she led him down their lane toward her favorite childhood walks, sharing young memories. They both avoided the subject of what would happen next.

Later that evening she brought him a glass of white wine to the patio.

"I never thought I would be drinking this. I was so resolved to stay in my rut all those years. Change feels good, thanks to you," London complimented.

"I'm sorry I told you that you were too settled."

"I was. I let my life engulf me and refused to see what I could be. You brought this out in me."

"I think we worked on it together. When I saw you at the bar that day, I was definitely intrigued. Then I found out you were a detective. Now I know that it was good you came into my life."

"I am dying to know," he hesitated. "Where do you see us at?"

"As much as I would like to be a part of your life and contribute to your happiness, I can't do that."

"I see. I kind of knew that you couldn't belong to anyone. You mentioned a while ago that you had to be free." He took her hand and she squeezed back and her heart began to break.

"It's not like I never thought about us being together. We were good. But I care about you too much to give myself to you. You deserve to be with someone who can give you a family and a future. I would fail at that."

"You could never fail at giving me anything. I understand how you feel. It would take me a long time to get over you."

She tilted her head and gave a sad look. Her eyes wanted to weep knowing what must be done.

"I will never forget you, Simone Harlow."

"Neither will I, London Taylor."

The two hugged and she began to cry, feeling the power in his embrace. He held her with so much feeling. London wanted to take her scent with him. Her fragrance stayed with him in his mind from the day she broke into his home. Her smile, her touch, her comical banter, the way she bravely and forcefully stood her ground. He loved all of it. It was an impossible obstacle. He must leave Italy without her.

He called the airline to confirm a flight that evening. His bags were packed and waiting at the front door. A taxi would arrive soon to rip him away from the one person he longed to be with.

"I still have your perfume on my clothes. Would it be silly to never have them dry cleaned?"

"Yes, but I think that it's endearing."

"I'll miss you."

"I'll miss you too."

The taxi pulled up and he grabbed his luggage and headed out the door.

"Oh, I forgot to give this to you."

He handed her a box and she opened it. Inside was a necklace with one diamond in the center.

"I want to give this to you. Wear it when you perform in front of those diplomats and kings." He could barely get the words out, "Something to remember me by."

"I love it. I'll wear it."

As he turned, she got in front of him and kissed him, pressing into him more intimately than before. She wanted this one to count and last.

"Goodbye, Simone."

He got into the cab and vanished. She entered her bedroom, box in hand. Pushing back the curtain and opening her window, she was taken back as a teenage girl who lived life without a care in the world. She had discovered that there was so much to care about and light finally came in. The one person she cared for most was London Taylor.

Chapter 13

Somehow You Will Find Your Way

London was dropped off at his apartment. It seemed odd to walk in and realize it as his home. He had been away long enough to forget. Looking around, he pictured Simone sitting on the couch with him and KB. At least, he still had his cat, thanks to Sully. He decided that he did not like his place anymore. It wasn't really him. Everything had changed and he needed to grow into his new life. What would that mean? His mind kept taking him back to days living with his parents. His parent's home, that would be a stretch. Simone would encourage him to try something new. London felt a weak desire to go there on his own without someone holding his hand. It was a good time to call Sully.

"London, I'm so glad you came home safe," Sully replied.

"Yeah, me too. It was incredible over there but... well, coming home just doesn't feel right either."

"What do you mean?"

"I no longer belong here. I need to go to my parent's home."

"That's a big step."

"It is, and I want to go there alone."

"Are you sure? The last time we talked about this, you wanted me to come along."

"I know but I have been through so much lately and it has given me enough courage to go by myself."

"What happened to the young woman, Penny Rose?"

"Oh, found out her name is really Simone. She still has to find her own life."

"Wasn't she in love with you?"

"I think she was. I definitely fell for her. She had to let us go."

"Did she give you a reason?"

"It doesn't matter what the reason is. She always has to do what's best for her."

"Are you brokenhearted?"

"No. I'm happy for her. I'll be fine."

Sully could sense how much London had grown. He was familiar with the case from the newspaper and TV. When he heard London was shot, it sent a chill through his body, fearing his friend might not return home. He could see him beginning a new chapter in his life and that was the good news he wanted to hear.

"Well, if you need me, just holler. I'll be here for you," affirmed Sully.

"Thanks, I'll pick up the cat later today."

London was feeling the jet lag and needed some rest. He still wasn't ready to go back to work. He noticed a lot of unanswered messages and mail to look through. He couldn't think about that right now. Gathering his thoughts about going to the house were on his mind.

After a few days of rest, London dug into a tin box and located the keys to the house. While he made his bed, KB stood in middle and rubbed his neck on his hands.

"Did you miss me, boy? Yeah, you did. If I feed you, will let me make this bed in peace?"

The dishes in the sink needed to be washed and he poured the flat beer down the sink. Drying the glasses, he thought about making an overdue phone call to the newspaper to stop sending the paper to his address. It felt good to keep up on the house and put something away after it was used. He saw the keys on the counter and gave a little hesitation. What was holding him back? He thought he was done grieving. Maybe it wasn't grief. Maybe it was fear of what it would be like to walk down the hallway or enter the living room. He grew up there and there was nothing wrong with the place. Whatever the reason, he knew he had to make a move.

As he started his car, he noticed on the passenger floorboard a lipstick case. It had to belong to Simone. He picked it up, recollecting the day she wore it.

"Excuse me, I need to go to the ladies room."

184

"Okay."

She took out her lipstick from her clutch and opened a small mirror.

"Lovely as can be. You don't need a mirror to see your beauty."

"I'm checking my lipstick. I have to go on in ten minutes."

"You can put it on right here. I like your company."

"Ease up, boy. When I'm on stage, it all has to be perfect."

"It can't get better than it already is."

He clutched it tight before tossing it in his glove box.

He pulled up in the driveway confidently. He wouldn't park across the street this time, like before. As always, he inspected the exterior, making sure the maintenance was working. The grass was lush, hydrangeas were blooming, trees were trimmed. and the walkway was cleaned of debris and leaves. The paint on the outside of the house still looked good. He reached into his pocket and pulled out the keys. He could hear them jingle as his hand slightly shook out the anxiety. Sliding the key into the lock, he turned it easily and left them hang.

With the house being shut up for years, it gave off a faint musty smell. Light dust showed on the coffee table and end tables. There were a few cobwebs near the shutters. He opened them to let in some natural light. Everything was still tidy and in its place. No dirty dishes or dirty laundry. His mother was always on top of that. Their couch was

185

still covered in plastic to keep it looking new, a pet peeve of his when he came to visit. His father's recliner was worn and the arms were slightly dirty. He could picture his father eating in front of the TV, dropping crumbs, and grabbing the arms to raise himself out. There was a rip in the seat that was never repaired. The kitchen was around the corner. She made her kitchen look like something he'd seen in Germany with busy wallpaper in the eating nook. His mother loved displaying her Portmeirion and Spode dishes. She only put up with his dad's collection of mugs with humorous sayings.

Down the hall, toward their bedroom was surreal and emotional to hear in his mind all of the commotion that went on in these rooms. Her white lace comforter covered their bed with pink and peach colored pillows. His father never appreciated her decor but loved his wife more since it made her happy. He opened the dresser drawer to see color coordinated shirts, pressed to perfection by his mother. He was a stickler for clean socks. If his white socks had stains that the washer didn't get out, he would buy new ones. His old bedroom still had his twin bed in the corner with a homemade quilt on top. They stored some boxes in there and a few of Allison's mother's things after she died. There was also an exercise bike against the wall that became a clothes hanger when not in use. Touching their things and opening the photo album was beautiful. The VCR would play a home movie he found. He was motivated to push play. It made him laugh at some of those times and shed tears, expressing happiness. Sitting in his father's chair, London remembered one unforgettable day.

"Allie, When's dinner ready? I'm starved."

"You are not starved. You could stand to lose a few pounds."

"Your cooking is to blame for that."

"London, wash up for dinner."

"Okay, Mom."

"Did you see what that boy brought home yesterday? A frog. I found it in the sink with a pile of rocks," complained Allison.

"Oh, he's being a boy. He hates to see anything hurt. He wants to save every living creature. That's my boy."

"Yes, your boy. Forget that I carried him for nine months."

"I will never forget that day."

John put the paper on the stand and got out of his chair. His wife was still recollecting.

"That was the happiest day of my life. After all those miscarriages, I never thought we'd get to be parents."

Just as London came into the kitchen, he saw his parents in a warm embrace and his father kissing his mother. It made him happy to see they were still in love, even if they were older.

The house was not exactly as he remembered, smaller, of course. The rooms were just memories now and it was time for London to make new ones in this place. Opening the garage door, he noticed his father's tools next to a collection of screws and different sized nails. He only needed one hammer but somehow ended up with four. He remembered his father showing him the great deal he got at a garage sale and hearing his mother say, *"You will never use it!"* and then whisper to his son, *"He already has twenty of the same thing sitting in that garage."* His mother's car was all that was parked inside. He could see a cup still in its holder advertising her favorite coffee shop. He noted how they took good care of it, and everything they had was still in remarkable shape. Unlike his father's car. He recalled going to the junk yard to find their mangled car in horrific condition. He cringed. It was awful, but not as bad as seeing them lying next to each other when they were pronounced dead. It was worse than a bad dream.

They did take good care of their place and they took good care of London. They worked hard to teach him things and values and humor and what did they expect from him? What would they want for him? Not wallowing in sorrow and mourning their death all his life. They created a happy home. He had to find a place in his own heart to help him push forward. The house was his best answer. As painful as it was walking through, it was actually good for him. London could feel his pain decrease, being replaced with wonderful memories and values. Two years and it was finally his time to move on.

London text Sully, *"I did it. I am moving on."*

Sully texted back, *"I knew you could. You are too good a man to shrink into a hole."*

He stayed in the house for a few hours longer and found himself not wanting to leave. He belonged there. He would make arrangements to move in as soon as his lease was up, in the next sixty days. Until then, each time he visited, he felt like they were there with him. For now, he would keep their furniture until he could sort out his emotions.

188

Chapter 14

Living Separate Lives

It had been five years since the trial. London's first steps to being on his own had changed him for the better. He knew who was and where he was going. The house his parents left him was remodeled and updated with new cabinets, appliances, and wood floors. He enjoyed life in a familiar place as his childhood home. It fit him just right. He never really cared for gardening so he continued to keep the gardeners on. He sold the furniture and donated most of their things, with the exception of his mother's china and a few keepsakes. He had an addition built to widen the garage, providing a place to keep his mother's car. He built a butcher block workbench at the end where he proudly displayed his father's favorite tools.

With a new outlook on life, London reached out for a new career. He was able to get a position at the local elementary school. First graders loved his teaching style and enthusiasm. He sold the investigating business to Berkely and never looked back. That part of his past was over and he focused on more important things. The house was paid for and he kept the deed in a safe place. It was his claim that kept his feet solid. KB found a new friend, a white Persian he named Italics. Life felt good. Passing by his parents' photo in the hallway, he smiled at how incredibly blessed he was to have been their son.

"Love you both," he whispered.

In the quiet of the evening, a soft knock was heard on the door.

"Simone."

"Hello, London."

"This is a surprise. Come in."

"I wanted to surprise you. How are you?"

Astonished, he closed the door behind her.

"I'm good. You got my new address. Wow, it's good to see you."

He tried to hold back his enthusiasm.

She noticed toys on the floor and noises coming from the bedroom.

"Oh, is someone here?"

"Yes, my wife."

"Oh, you're married?"

"Yes and expecting a new baby soon." His wife appeared from the hallway.

London kissed her and took their son in his arms.

"Simone, this is Wendy and our son, Jaxson."

"It's nice to meet you," Simone said politely.

"London has told me all about you. It's so nice to finally meet you."

She was feeling a bit awkward. She never expected London to be married or a father.

Jaxson was getting fussy and Wendy took a hold of him.

"I'm sorry. We're getting ready for a bath and bedtime. I'll be back soon." Wendy excused herself.

"She's beautiful."

"We met at school. She's a teacher just like me."

"So you're not a detective anymore. Why didn't you tell me that?"

"I was focused on Wendy and the baby. We work at the elementary school west of here. It just gives us a lot of joy to shape young minds. We love being teachers."

"I'm glad you're happy."

"So, what have you been up to?"

"I came here to tell you that I'm singing with an orchestra now. They offered me a chance I couldn't refuse, and I'm loving it. I also came here to spend some time with Joe. He's getting older and he needs me to be there for him. He finally decided to move to Italy. Kind of like a lifelong roommate. When I told him a few years ago about the trial and what this has done for me, he was proud of me."

"Have you found anyone yet? I mean, did you ever fall in love?"

"No. I've had offers but no one I'm settled on. Maybe when I'm older, I'll need someone to help me tie my shoes or bring me dinner. But retirement is too far away and I love what I do."

"I remember you telling me that someday I would find happiness and I think I've have found it. I fell for Wendy and discovered where I was meant to be." He thought about Andrew and Evelyn.

"How are your parents?"

"They're good. They ask about you sometimes. They finally retired and moved to Greece. He's always wanted to retire there. They live next to a villa with a small view of the ocean."

"Do you still remember that old place I used to call home?"

"That apartment? The first time I saw it, I thought only a guy could live in there."

"Yeah, the one you broke into. I don't even know that person anymore."

"London, I'm glad you finally made it here. I know life had been rough on you."

"It was at first. I'm glad I made the move. It was worth it and brought me back to where I belonged. The hardest thing I ever did was step back in this house."

"That was harder than saving me?" she smirked.

"I never imagined I would have such a fulfilling life with Wendy. You were very hard to get over but I knew where you were headed and respected that."

"I have to be honest. I was falling for you and I missed you so much. I picked up the phone so many times to call you home to Italy and stay with me. I knew it was only a fleeting idea and would end in sorrow. Seeing you now, I know we made the right decision."

"We are both in a good place and I am proud of your success. Sometimes I wonder what it would have been like if we solved crimes together. We'd be the new super heroes in our own comic book."

She laughed, "That's an idea. We would have made a great team. The man who never stepped on my toes during a dance."

London missed her banter. After giving her the tour, he asked her to stay for dinner. The three of them sat outside on the deck beside a blazing fire. Wendy laced her fingers around a cup of herbal tea while London sipped wine. Simone never changed her choice of drink, always red wine. When the night had ended, it was time to say goodbye. Wendy and London both enjoyed her company and invited her back anytime she was in the area. After she stepped out the door, London stopped her on the walk.

"Simone."

"Yes."

"What is your stage name now or do you have one?"

"Just Simone. Penny Rose no longer exists."

"I miss her."

"I miss her too."

They hugged as friends, knowing their lives had entangled for those few months to make the world right again. As she waved a last goodbye, he closed the door and opened his computer to looked her up. There she was with tour dates throughout Europe. She never had to reach far for the stars. It came to her naturally. He could never forget the woman with the potential to make anything possible.

Adventurous, sultry, sensual, and undeniably beautiful. For London Taylor, the former agent would be in his memory forever as the songstress, Miss Penny Rose.

Penny Rose

Annette Marie Stephenson

2023

Other Books By Annette Stephenson

Divided Mountain

The Landscaper's Wife
The Continued Story of Divided Mountain

The Tree at Lindley Park

The Other Side of Brook

The Glass Vase

The Shoe Box

The Last Memory

Made in the USA
Columbia, SC
28 August 2023